THE CHRISTMAS SALON

Clyve Rose

Boroughs
Publishing Group

www.BOROUGHSPUBLISHINGGROUP.com

PUBLISHER'S NOTE: This is a work of fiction. Names, characters, places and incidents either are the product of the author's imagination or are used fictitiously. Any resemblance to actual events, locales, business establishments or persons, living or dead, is coincidental. Boroughs Publishing Group does not have any control over and does not assume responsibility for author or third-party websites, blogs or critiques or their content.

THE CHRISTMAS SALON
Copyright © 2020 Clyve Rose

ISBN 978-1-953810-17-5

For Beautiful Bella, who always belongs to herself.
And for Mum, Dad, Danielle, Julie, Sara, & Alon:
The ones who catch you before you hit the ground never lose their wings.
Thank You. xxx

THE CHRISTMAS SALON

Chapter 1

Summer 1810
Grantchester Meadows, Cambridge

"Get to it, Musgrave." The ham-fisted shove might have sent Henry into the Cam.

"I'll not, Clifton, if it's all the same to you." Henry shook the senior fellow off, content to cool his bare feet in the shallows. A rustle nearby distracted him, but he was soon fending off the splashing antics of his university cohorts. He hovered close to the riverbank, reaching into his fob pocket more than once.

"Relax," his friend shouted again. "The bells will tell us when we're missed."

"Very well," he called back, ducking to protect his book from getting soaked. It was a fine day for larking about on the Cam. "My godfather and his daughter are coming down today," he added.

Wil Clifton surfaced nearby, hearing only the second part of this speech. "So you've told me at least a dozen times since the post's come. We will return in time, Musgrave. You have my word."

"I thank you."

"Are your visitors so intriguing? As your godfather's ward, surely you're acquainted with his family?"

"Yes, I grew up on the General's estate at Clayford. His daughter and I played together as children, though I've not met her for an age."

"Ah," Wil nodded sagely.

Henry bridled but said nothing. As a senior fellow, his friend had already enlisted. Henry had a year remaining in which to make up his mind as to his career. That's if his godfather didn't make it up for him. Cupping his hand, Henry let the water flow through his fingers and dampened his hair, scratching at his scalp.

"Miss Beresford is likely much altered," Wil talked on. "This explains your fascination."

"It is not a fascination," Henry protested. "It's simply..." He paused.

"Yes?"

"Well, she paints," he finished.

"All girls paint," his friend replied with a shrug.

"Not like Miss Beresford," Henry insisted, falling silent. He had no desire to create a fascination regarding Louisa, especially with a Clifton.

"Her *art* is what fascinates you?" Wil sounded incredulous.

"Yes, and it is *not* a fascination," Henry repeated.

Wil arced a practised brow. "Come, Musgrave, it is very little less. Is she out?"

"Not at all," Henry hastened to assure him. "They journey from here for her Season."

"Excellent." The older boy slapped Henry's shoulder so vehemently he barely avoided tumbling face-first into the current again.

Henry righted himself moments later, winded, and nearly bereft of his reading material. When he bent over to regain his breath, he noticed a pair of eyes directly opposite his own and could have sworn he heard a sharp intake of breath. As soon as he blinked, the eyes disappeared. Another gasp—a *feminine* gasp—reached his ears, followed by much softer scratching. He froze in astonishment.

Like his friends, he'd come here for a bathe. Apart from himself, who'd stripped merely to his linen, the rest of his friends were all splendidly nude young men. Henry was caught. Should he alert the others? Or investigate? Another rustle and he shot out an arm, grabbing what felt like a youthful shoulder.

"What do you think you're do—" and then, "*Louisa*?"

Henry backed up rapidly, soaking his breeches to the hips. Not much of a swimmer, this was enough to spark tension. Behind him, Clifton retreated to the opposite bank, shouting for the others to dress and depart. Henry ignored his fellows' bawdy farewells as he attended to the matter—the *woman*—before him. He took another step into deeper waters.

"You'll not tell the General?" were the first words from her lips.

"Give me one good reason why I shouldn't," he replied, while his mind attempted to calculate how much this precocious chit might have seen—and how to banish the image of tumbling auburn curls falling haphazardly around her prettily flushed face from his mind.

"Where is Uncle George?" He looked around.

"Attending some ancient acquaintance," Louisa answered with a saucy grin. "His friend assisted us in arriving with an earlier post. I made my escape while I was able, hoping to sketch bathers by the millpond."

"But you've seen—"

"Barely anything at all," Louisa replied airily. "To own the truth, I was too shy for a proper viewing."

"*A proper*—" Henry could hardly speak for shock. "There is nothing proper about this behaviour, and you know it." He attempted to imbue his tone with dignity, but the expression on Louisa's face was endearing. Half fright, half fearlessness—and all bewilderment. He bit the insides of his cheeks to prevent a grin.

"What did you think you were doing?" he managed finally.

"I've not only come to visit with *you*, dear Henry," she retorted as if this explained everything.

"With whom then?" He did nothing to soften the hard edge in his voice.

"With my Muse." Facing away from him, she continued sketching furiously.

"What is it you mean, Louisa?"

"How else am I to learn the male form?" Louisa protested. "Not even you will sit for me."

"Whom have you asked?"

"Whom may I ask, with propriety?" Her blush belied her indignation as he pretended offense. Henry watched the amber lights enliven the depths of her eyes as she turned her flushed face to his. She wore her most beguilingly charming smile.

"Oh, Henry, will you?" Her tone implied he could bestow no greater gift.

It was quite impossible to be angry with her after that.

Henry held her lit-up gaze with his as he climbed out of the river, walked back to the rocks, and untied his shirt. She was already studying light and shape, seemingly immune to all other sensation. *Which makes one of us.*

The distance between them was decent. Had she been one of his college fellows, there'd not have been the slightest impropriety about sketching by the riverbank in high summer, but she wasn't a Cambridge art fellow. She was his godfather's daughter; she was Louisa. Her darting looks to and fro were art, not coquetry.

Henry's disappointment shocked him. Seated as she was, he could not estimate her height but she'd grown prettier and filled out a good deal in his absence from Clayford. His eyes took in her softly rounded shape. She was generously breasted, the gentle slope of her shoulders leading to her elegant neck and those auburn curls he remembered. It wasn't easy, remaining still and poised with nothing to look upon but this pretty woman. Pretty? No. *Louisa is beautiful.*

"I've not seen you so still before," he teased, daring to smile.

"I'll thank you not to distract me, Henry, if you can manage it." Her tone gentled. "It's too good of you to allow me this chance, considering that hiding in the cupboard of your life drawing class will see me branded a hoyden."

Henry swivelled his head in shock, eliciting a groan of frustration from his artist. "Would you truly do such a thing, simply to gaze upon a man?"

"Would I not? For art's sake, I will do what I must." She shrugged, letting out a deep sigh. "It is not prurience. How else do you suggest I improve my rendering of masculine figures?"

Henry stifled a suggestive laugh. "My responses are unfit for a lady's ears, Louisa."

To Henry's delight, she blushed as he spoke. Her head lifted, her face nearly solemn except for the softest shake of her head. "You've moved again. Please return to the pose exactly, or I am ruined forever as a figure painter."

"If it keeps you from spying on my college fellows, I can't pretend to be sorry," he replied, immediately contrite at the bruised quality in her eyes.

Louisa remained silent for a long moment, her gaze flicking between her page and her model. "A half-turn of your head towards me, dear Henry."

He dutifully rearranged himself. "Like so?"

"A narrower turn, if you'd be so good."

He obeyed.

Seemingly satisfied, she nodded. "It is precisely as it was. Thank you."

He held himself quite still, listening to her soft humming. It was a moment unlike any he'd experienced up to that point, in all his eighteen years of life. Sunshine on his shoulders, the skin of his back resting casually against the solid tree trunk behind him. He was sure there were birds, or bees, or even wasps pollinating the riverbank, but Henry was aware only of softly scratching chalk and the quiet sounds falling from Louisa's lips. Now pursed in concentration, her lips appeared as lovely as he remembered. He couldn't help wondering if she recalled their first kiss as he did, remembering a shared moment on another riverbank. The day she'd risked her life to save his, and afterward…the press of her girlish mouth on his cheek, her lips opening to his. *Her lips…*

He remembered all of it—the pinking of her sweet mouth with his, her gasp, his hesitation after she'd pulled him from the water. With his departure the next day, Louisa's weekly letters had guarded him against homesickness. In the end, all he missed at Cambridge was *her*. He studied the softly feminine shape, honing his focus. Henry wished he might shift positions, to learn her form as closely as she examined his.

"Your patience is appreciated." She spoke after a time, distracting him from more dangerous imaginings. "You're rather good at this."

"Thank you," Henry barely replied.

She looked up at the oddness of his speech, uttered through immobilised lips. "I beg your pardon, Henry, it's past an hour." Laying down her materials, she gazed up at him, entirely relaxed, at peace with herself and her world. "Must you return to your college?"

A pretty young woman, skilled and at work beneath such a sky, on a day when the Cam sparkled with light and the shade of the old tree screening them as they sat on the grassy green bank…it was enough for Henry to say, "Not yet, if you do not wish it."

"I shall have done in a moment." Her quick glance skimmed from her page to him and back again several more times. He saw her add her initials with a flourish. "If you need to move now, it will not ruin this."

Move he duly did, re-dressing his torso until he was far more formal and far less comfortable, especially in his wet-through breeches. Still, perhaps that was best, given the currents of his thoughts.

"You are so good to sit for me above an hour." Louisa spoke over her shoulder as he stood behind her, settling his collar and cravat. "Do you not have lectures?"

"Not today," Henry lied. He cleared his throat as his gaze drifted to where her curls parted over the back of her neck. Her creamy skin appeared almost translucent below the ribbons of her bonnet. Reaching out to touch her, he caught himself, taking up her work instead. Excellent execution aside, the girl's pictures would make a Frenchman blush. There was no ordered composition, nor any formality of design. His cheeks heated as he considered that covert peeping in the name of art was hardly a formal process. Then again, considering the state of his breeches, formality was clearly not in order today. He studied her sketches, noting the angled lines creating an illusion of depth. Astonishment struck him speechless a moment.

"Why, your work is outstanding," he declared at last.

Louisa stood, taking up her sketchbook as she did so. "You are very kind, Henry."

"Kindness has nothing to do with it," he replied. "I have studied here for many months to attempt art—but you, you succeed, Louisa. Is it possible you are unaware of this?"

"The General—" Louisa began and fell silent.

"It is true, Uncle George has no appreciation for art, and you've spent all your time at Clayford, but you are in town for the Season. You ought to have the benefit of a London master. It may assist your coming out." Henry frowned because this idea seemed suddenly unpleasant. He stared at the sketches in her hand. "I shall speak to my godfather directly," he promised.

"What will a master seek to teach me?" Louisa asked after a moment. "Will I learn figure painting, like this?"

Henry glanced at her without moving his head. "Not like this, I assure you." He grinned at such an idea. "Female figure painting, certainly. You will also learn technique, consistency, the basic skills of composition and colour. Skill *can* be learned. Talent is innate, and you are talented, Louisa. Truly." He spoke forcefully, doing all in his power to convey his conviction.

Henry looked from the picture to Louisa, pleased at the pride shining in her face, the amber light in the depths of her brown eyes when she delighted in some small thing. Her art, however, was no minor object. He knew excellence when he saw it, and Louisa's work met that definition.

"Not one—not a single one of my fellow daubers—could match the work you have performed here in a single afternoon."

"Credit is due the model as well, is it not?" she replied, half-jesting. "Sitting for a likeness is not so easy as some imagine. You are quite skilled yourself."

Henry shook his head emphatically, determined to make his point. "Not so skilled as you."

She glanced up at him before refocusing on her work. "I am not sure I captured your mouth. Is it like?"

Leaning down, he lifted her hand to his lips without lowering his head. His gaze on her sweet eyes, Henry pressed his mouth to her knuckles. Tracing his lips with one hesitant finger, she sighed and smiled. He tried smiling back but his mouth seemed stilled. He couldn't breathe, forgetting how. He tongued her fingertip, tasting chalk. Placing her arm about his neck, he lowered his mouth firmly over her lips…and oh, the sweet intoxication, like pears and honeyed wine, her lips as warm in life as in memory, in dreams. As warm as Louisa herself, gazing up at him with her intense, amber-brown gaze, opening to him as he rested one hand on her hip, the other cradling her cheek reverently. He might be drunk on such heady refreshment, and now Henry knew she wanted him.

He deepened his kiss, pulling her gently closer, his palm tightening at her waist. He made no demands with his mouth and no promises with his body. He didn't press her against him, did not torment her with his desire. In this moment, it was enough to taste her, to know her in this fresh, enticing way, to learn Louisa anew.

Her hesitant response grew bolder, her lips welcoming, the shift of her breasts against his waistcoat making him wild. It pained him to take his mouth from hers, to lean back and stroke her cheek softly, smiling at the most becoming blush she'd ever sported. He didn't speak. Neither did she, those expressive eyes of hers alight before him. There was trust there, admiration, and a flattering awareness he dared not credit.

"Louisa," he breathed, as the bells of St John's heralded the dinner hour.

His fair artist started in his arms, those perfect eyes widening with alarm. "Henry, the General! We are late." Shoving her sketches into his hands, she gathered up her box of chalks before hitching her skirts slightly to run headlong back up the path to his college hall.

Henry stood there a moment, watching her racing up the hillside, away from his kiss. *I am not sure I captured your mouth…*

He followed slowly, refusing to smile, unwieldy sensations flowing through him. Desire, regard, and a kind of fear he thought he understood.

Oh, Louisa, if you knew my heart.

Henry met with the General that evening. The next day, he withdrew from Cambridge, enlisting for his godfather's regiment.

Chapter 2

August 1814
Madame Vignée's apartments at the Louvre, Paris

Louisa twisted into something resembling a knotted skein as she attempted to achieve the perspective demanded of her.

"*Précisémont!*" Madame Vignée exclaimed, turning back to the canvas mounted on her easel. "Now, the breast, *mon coeur.*"

Barely flinching, Louisa drew the sheer fabric to one side as her infant took her nipple in his mouth. Biting her tongue to stifle a momentary gasp of pain, she held as still as she was able, relaxing as little Henri uttered the gurgling sounds of satisfaction Louisa had learned to appreciate.

"I cannot hold this position for long, Madame," Louisa warned, moving her lips as little as possible. Her son was a distractible child, but she'd rather feed Henri herself than hire a wet nurse as her mother had done. Besides, Louisa did not have the francs.

"It is long enough," the artist assured her. "I need simply a sense of this scene for my *Madone*, and then you may step down. It is so much better for realism to draw it this way."

True to her word, in less time than Louisa would have been able to capture such a design, Madame Vignée drew the sitting to a close. The paintwork was intimate and intricate, even capturing the tiny dimpling on Henri's thighs. Louisa smiled in true admiration, reflecting how fortunate she was to have one of the first women artists admitted to *l'Académie* as her teacher.

"*Merci*, Louisa." Madame Vignée reached for her reticule.

Louisa shook her head. "I am already indebted to you, Madame," she insisted. "We live in your *le Louvre* rooms."

"Ah, *mon amie*, you must be more mercenary," her tutor replied. "You have the little one to consider. Besides, once Traversant is admitted to *l'Académie*, he will make me famous with your work. I feel it *here*." The older woman tapped her palette knife lightly over her left breast.

Louisa glowed with pleasure. "You are already famed across the continent, Madame. Neither the Bonapartes nor the Bourbonnes refuse you."

Madam Vignée's vanity allowed her a smile but she did not blush. Nodding in the direction of the drapery covering the other part of their shared studio, she laughed. "You flatter me, Louisa, and I do not mind it. Nevertheless, these are not easy times for art, *mon amie*. I, too, flatter whom I must, and let us not discuss the Bonapartes. There are far too many rumours. How is your admission piece coming along? May I see it?"

Louisa offered her an arch smile. "*Non*, Madame. My teacher insists I do not exhibit incomplete work. And you know, she is an artful woman."

Her companion threw her turbaned head back, laughing until tears beaded in her eyes. "*Mon Dieu*, I will never understand how a man could be so foolish as to let you go. Though in truth, men *are* fools." Gazing seriously at Henri, she tucked a handful of coins into Louisa's palm. "His loss is *le Louvre*'s gain."

Louisa could not quite smile at this. "I hope so. Or at least, *l'Académie*'s. My admission piece for Monsieur Traversant is but half complete."

Her friend made a tutting noise in her throat. "Always, you are so uncertain, dear Louisa. You have a gift—a very great gift. The Muse speaks through you, and you must heed this truth." Madame Vignée sighed again, heavily. "All art is, is truth."

She cooed at the babe before gathering her cloak. "We will find your Cupid, Louisa." "Good evening, *ma chère amie*. I must visit my vicomte, and he will not wait long. He is barely twenty-three." She winked at Louisa's laughter. "Scandalous, am I not?"

Louisa shook her head, blushing for her friend. "Indeed, Madame, yet I do not know what we should do without you." She stood to help the older woman with her cloak, glad it was not she sallying out into the streets of Paris with such a wind about. "Please take care, Madame." She hugged her tight, kissing both her cheeks. "*Bonne nuit*."

After Madame left, Louisa's thoughts focused on dinner, speculating whether the fruit that formed part of her still life was spoiled, or if she might like to consume such for her evening meal. *The latter, for who knows when I might afford grapes again?* She ate, doing her best to avoid the pile of forwarded correspondence at her elbow. More remonstrance from the General would not aid her digestion. Straightening her spine, she turned resolutely away from her unopened letters.

England was her past. Paris was *now*—and her future? Louisa sighed. Her future had no shape yet, but her present was not so dire as it might once have been. Christmas in a Paris blessed with peace after so much uncertainty must be a joyful celebration, even if her family had cast her off. *Not Henry*, she amended with a twinge of guilt. Her old playfellow from Clayford still wrote regularly, wondering at her lack of response. Louisa blinked back tears as she watched over Henri, named for the General's godson instead of the boy's true father.

Smiling down at her child, she mentally counted her blessings: a roof over their heads and good friends were more than many people had in Paris.

"We even have grapes," she said to her sleeping babe, plucking another morsel and savouring the taste against her tongue. After her meagre fare, Louisa drew aside the sheet covering an enormous looking glass that took up one entire wall of her home and studio. Lighting her treasured Sevres lamp, she took up her sketch brush. Louisa removed her wrap and arranged herself supine on a divan placed there for the purpose. She followed the lines of her flesh with her eyes, planning her next strokes. One-handed, and with careful, deft movements, Louisa continued her study of the female form in repose.

***

December 1814
Baron von Humboldt's parlour
Vienna

"France claims it is not withholding treasures from the Papal States." Baron von Humboldt looked up from his correspondence with a cynical smile. "What say you to this, Major Musgrave?"

Henry returned the Prussian's smile. "I say we both know a well-crafted piece of fiction when we read such," he replied calmly. "Talleyrand is well aware that the *Triumphal Quadriga* belongs to the Church. Not to the French Republic." *Which no longer exists.*

"The French diplomat is slippery," the baron said carefully. "I hear he attends us at Metternich's assembly this evening."

Henry raised his brows. "He may dance with us or not, baron. It changes nothing. France must return the missing works. Our allies insist on this, and their patience is not limitless." He did his best to maintain a veneer of calm. The prevarication of the French was enough to put him in a temper, especially when he considered the value of the art they'd looted from the rest of Europe. He noticed that his host bore such insolence better.

"As an acknowledged collector this is a good assignment, though I do not like to travel in the winter. Is it so for you as well, Major?"

"It is more welcome to winter in your halls than in the army officer's quarters," Henry answered as the baron's footman refilled his glass. "Your hospitality is much appreciated."

The baron inclined his head. "It is a pleasure to have your company, Major. I enjoy debating art with you. It is far more interesting than politics."

"Certainly," Henry agreed.

"I would wish to present my betrothed to you while you dine here." His host's tone was unapologetically complacent. "Rebecca cannot accompany us to Paris for *Le Salon de Noël*. This is my last Christmas as a bachelor gentleman, I fear."

"You do not seem to fear it, my friend. You rather appear delighted, which is fitting. I wish you joy."

"I thank you," the baron replied. "Rebecca attends Metternich's assembly this evening. For one night, we may forget politics and enjoy the dancing, and art, and the ladies of my acquaintance. Will it do?"

"Your hospitality overwhelms me, baron." Henry sipped his drink.

The baron's gaze narrowed. "Hmmm…but I perceive you do not wish to dance with my lady Rebecca? I assure you, Major, I am relying on you for this. My war service left me lame, as you know." The baron stretched his wounded leg, attempting a sorrowful expression that had Henry laughing in a moment.

"It will be my honour to dance with your lady Rebecca," he replied. "I must beg your pardon. I confess I am thinking too often of attending *Le Salon de Noël* than my current engagements at our congress."

The baron nodded enthusiastically. "As am I, Major. The first exhibit for almost a decade will be a sight to behold, will it not?"

"It will be a Christmas to remember," Henry replied, his eyes straying to his extensive correspondence, lest the baron read his expression too well. "How long might a missive from Prussia take to reach us here?"

Von Humboldt shrugged. "From where in Prussia precisely? From my Berlin residence, it is not more than five days."

"And from Cologne?"

The baron shook his head. "The post from towns closer to the wars is not so good. You are concerned?"

"I confess I am," Henry replied. "I have acquaintance resident in your homeland, sent there for safety several months ago." He swallowed. "I've not received replies to my last letters."

"As soldiers, we assume the worst. This does not make it so, Major. The reliability of post from the towns bordering France is not as it was." His friend uttered a heartfelt sigh as he stretched his maimed limb again. "Like so much else."

Henry acknowledged this truth with a nod. "I am sure you're right. The explanation is likely simple enough."

He dared not discuss the matter further. He'd not set eyes on Louisa since Cambridge, but their correspondence had been unreserved and utterly delightful to him. *Had been*…beneath the table, Henry unclenched his palm, trying to ignore the tension in his muscles. He recalled the day he'd learned of Louisa's circumstances. The General's stricken face haunted him still.

Seeing his host studying him again, Henry managed a faint smile. Politics left little time for inward reflection, and tomorrow's post may allay his fears. Tonight, he was expected to make merry with drinking and dancing, which was no hardship. Outmanoeuvring the French in matters of art required patience and politeness. Sighing, Henry rose with a bow, excusing himself to dress.

In truth, he had little need to prepare. Baker was the kind of aide-de-camp who required no oversight of any kind, except in the field. Henry's brushed jacket hung ready by the armoire, his decorations freshly polished and shining by lamplight. Once attired for dinner, Henry began his report for the Embassy, detailing the day's tricky negotiations and the new rumours regarding Bonaparte. Baker's knock at the sitting-room door came a little later.

"A hack awaits you, sir. The baron is already down."

Henry nodded and stood, stretching, before following his man downstairs. Baker waited by the hack, Henry's caped officer's coat open and ready.

"Thank you." Henry donned the coat, smiling absently as he seated himself beside the baron. Leaning forward, he charged his aide, "Should any message arrive from the Embassy, send for me at once."

Baker nodded. "From the Embassy. Understood, Major."

"Or Cologne," Henry added.

"Cologne?" his host repeated. "Your correspondent still concerns you, Major?"

Henry nodded, staring out of the window. *Always.*

***

He'd scarcely bowed his introduction to von Humboldt's lady before Talleyrand's man accosted him. Their entire exchange over the past week had been a study in light and shade.

"I bring no news of the artworks you requested," the Frenchman declared, waving Henry's letter before him like a battle standard. "We do not possess these pieces."

"It's as well that their recovery falls to England and Prussia then, and not to France," Henry valiantly resisted tapping the other man's smug visage with his fist. *Hasn't anyone told you that France lost the wars?*

"Come, Major." His French counterpart hardly bowed as the music floated across to them. "The dances are beginning and I promised my wife the first waltz. Will you not join us to dine?"

Barely refraining from rolling his eyes, Henry stepped around him, nodding.

"Everyone is aware that the *grande armée* looted these artistic treasures," he commented, adjusting his cravat. He waited until his counterpart opened his mouth to protest, before bowing again and offering his arm to the lady Rebecca at last.

Taking his position on the dance floor, Henry kept one eye on the Frenchman. He would dance beside Talleyrand's envoy all night if need be, and he would succeed in the end. Bonaparte took the art because he could and because it was historical and valuable. In Henry's estimation, he did not understand the most important part of what he had stolen: Art *mattered.*

It certainly mattered to him, as his antidote to the often solitary life of a soldier. Glancing down at his dance partner, he remembered it was his turn to speak.

"You dance divinely, dear lady."

"I thank you, Major." The girl coloured, looking twice as pretty. "Have the French given up their secrets?"

"I never discuss business with a lady," he replied smilingly, twirling her once. "I am able to admire your superior dancing, and your dress, of course."

His dance partner laughed. "I thank you. As von Humboldt's acquaintance, you may address me as he does. My sister accompanies us this evening. Eloise is less complimentary regarding the charm of English officers."

"I am sorry to hear it, lady Rebecca," he replied gravely, glancing at the dark-eyed beauty seated beside the baron. "I shall do what I'm able, in remedy." He smiled again, his face aching. "I am merely a poor major, you know."

The lady Rebecca laughed again. "So said von Humboldt before we were courting. You must own that being in love suits a man far more so than a woman." Seeing him shake his head, she went on. "You disagree? Come, Major, we shall see you give up the life of a lonely soldier one of these days, and what then will you have to say?"

Henry laughed politely, looking towards the baron. The Prussian grinned benignly at Henry waltzing with his betrothed. Lady Rebecca clearly loved to dance. Presumably, her sister was as attractively charming. Escorting Rebecca back to her party, he bowed.

"Good evening." He kissed her younger sister's glove as gallantly as he was able.

Henry watched his friend's eyes warm as he introduced his betrothed's family. "I thank you for your attentions, Major. I trust my lady Rebecca has not beguiled you too much?"

"Hardly," replied his lady, slipping her arm into the baron's. "He barely allowed me to flirt and resisted all encroachment on his six inches manfully." She gave a gay, giddy laugh to indicate she was unaffected.

The baron barely raised a brow. "I see her efforts are wasted, Major. So I am not offended."

"I should hope not," Henry replied earnestly, before collecting himself. "Your lady Rebecca is utterly charming." This was said with equal earnestness. After all, it was true.

"I thank you," the baron replied with a satisfied smile. "If there is one thing I recognise, Major, it's a man whose heart is already lost." He leaned in. "I would wish to know who this woman is who haunts you so. She is a fitting subject for an artist, no?"

Henry hardly knew how to reply. He feared he flushed, until slyly rescued by his dance partner.

"Come, come, Wilhelm. You forget the Major is English. We must not embarrass him."

"I am not embarrassed." Henry tried to appear as if this were true, staring uneasily around the assembly room. The discomfort he felt was not entirely cultural. He noted the grave faces seated beside the Duke of Wellington. The gaiety seemed forced in several quarters. An air of disquiet pervaded. Leaning in close, Baron von Humboldt spoke in an undertone.

"You sense it too, Major?"

"People *appear* at ease. I do not believe it to be genuine." He glanced again at Wellington. "We've heard rumours from Elbe."

The Prussian's expression remained inscrutable. "There are always rumours, Major." His tone lacked levity. Henry watched his eyes. *What do you know, my friend?*

Whatever Prussia's information, the baron was no more at liberty to discuss it than Henry was to speak of stolen artwork with the lady Rebecca. He exhaled slowly, accepting a drink from a server. Politics was an ugly business. He much preferred art.

"We'll not countenance another Bonaparte."

Heads turned to find the orator of such an impolitic declaration. Henry's shock evaporated when he saw it was Viscount Castlereagh. Squinting across the assembly room, Henry assessed the young diplomat. Castlereagh appeared to be in his cups, laughing with the newly arrived Papal participants, and paying little heed to the other diners observing his behaviour.

Henry rose abruptly. Catching the eye of Metternich's envoy, he inclined his head in apology, noting the other man's helpless shrug.

"Lady Rebecca, Miss Horsham, Baron, I do beg your pardon." He lifted each lady's hand, brushing his lips over finely worked gloves. "My urgent attendance is required elsewhere." He bowed, retreating from Lady Eloise's flattering smiles with what he hoped passed as his equally flattering sighs of regret. The girl had a superb figure and elegant manners, but she was young. He'd seen too much as a soldier to ever feel *young* again. Henry thanked God and England that the wars were over at last.

In any case, the General had not sent Major Musgrave to Vienna to find a wife. Henry's first duty was to secure the return of the "lost treasures" for England's allies. His godfather also charged him to "guard the viscount." The General's discretion prevented additional details, but Henry was well aware of the young man's imprudence.

"A breath of air, my lord?" He helped Castlereagh onto the terrace, where a member of the Prussian delegation suggested billiards. Henry spied Talleyrand's party setting up for cards—the very people with whom he was required to negotiate. The viscount was all in, and Castlereagh stumbled against him, throwing his arm around Henry's shoulders. Henry glanced back towards Talleyrand's people. *Blast!* Mentally consigning the bloody-minded French to the devil, he escorted the viscount to his Embassy residence, where he leaned on the bell and all but dropped the peer into the arms of the surprised butler.

He about-faced as quickly as possible, but by the time he returned, the French were not interested in discussing terms for their stolen artworks. *If they ever were.* Henry shrugged and made his farewells before arriving back at von Humboldt's town house. Seating himself at his escritoire, he completed his report. *Yes, the French have the artworks. No, they're not admitting to such. Yes, I will find out more.* After a little thought, he added a note suggesting the viscount be recalled to Westminster.

Henry sat there a moment, reluctant to head up to bed. His dreams had been strange of late, though no stranger than the restlessness that possessed him since the cessation of hostilities. He stood to gaze out his window. The baron's prospect over the

Volksgarten was inspiring and stabling for his horses ample. His host's proximity to the auction houses was another blessing. This restlessness had nothing to do with his accommodations. Perhaps he ought to try getting drunk. It seemed to work for most of his acquaintance.

As if on cue, his aide-de-camp knocked and entered, bearing the brandy decanter and a single glass. "Good evening, Major. How was tonight's ball?"

"Long, Baker. Far too long."

Baker mumbled under his breath in sympathy. "I've had a message from von Humboldt, who is not yet returned. He wishes to breakfast early tomorrow, and requested you join him 'to discuss art.'"

Henry cheered considerably. "Did you reply in the affirmative?"

"Knowing how you prefer art to politics, Major, I did so."

Henry sighed heavily. "Art is beautiful. Politics is ugly."

"And balls, sir?"

"Balls lie somewhere in between," Henry smiled at Baker's grunting laugh. "You may turn in yourself. Good night, Baker."

"Good night, sir."

Pouring out a small snifter of liquor, Henry finally took himself off to bed.

The looped vine swings from the old tree. The girl spies a flower at the end of a branch. The branch looks strong enough to his eyes; eyes that slowly notice the growing girl beside him. She sees the flower and her eyes light up like stars at night. The desire in the girl's face, her longing for beauty, enchants him. He climbs the tree, leaning towards the petals, the stalk. Stretching just that bit farther until the muscles beneath his skin tauten fully. He reaches, stretches, and with a sickening crack! he falls. The girl screams—

Henry's eyes opened in shock, heart beating as though it would force its way through flesh. He'd not dreamed so vividly in years. For a moment, he fancied a swinging vine before his waking eyes. Taking a deep breath, he blinked slowly. His room. His drawn drapes. Vienna. The Congress. No drowning. No river. No girl. *No Louisa.* Adjusting his pillows, he rolled over, falling rapidly back asleep.

Chapter 3

Louisa slit open the envelope that arrived with the dawn post. Impressively addressed to "Monsieur Traversant, Esq.," she had no intention of ignoring this note from the director of the Dorotheum:

November 1814
The Dorotheum, Vienna

Dear Monsieur Traversant,
I am delighted to inform you that after a mere five days' exhibition, all three of your works have received offers of sale. While no transactions are yet final, I expect excellent results from the Christmastide auction, especially for your portraits.
I remind you of our thirty percent fee. We provide a full accounting at the quarter day.
At your service,
Herr le Bruhn

Louisa could not restrain her delighted cheer.

"Oh." She glanced apprehensively at her son, but Henri slept on, oblivious. "Two sales of work shall see us through this holiday," she whispered. *Three, and I may have new gloves.*

She busied herself with warm water and bread, hoping some fruit remained in the stillroom. Suppressing a sigh for the days when she rose to chocolate served by a maid in the late morning, and a full repast of eggs and ham, she gave herself a determined shake. With a son to provide for and work to do, she had no time to spend reminiscing. Henri's sharp cry came as the church bells chimed for matins. Louisa swallowed the last of her breakfast and hurried to take care of her babe.

***

Breakfasting at the uncivilised hour of nine o'clock in the morning, Henry shook off his weariness and attended to his host.

"I thank you for breakfasting so early, Major," the baron said once the covers were all in place. "I heard a whisper at the assembly last night after your departure."

"Concerning?"

"There is a small *kunstgalerie* close by the Dorotheum. It's said to deal in the works we are seeking. The owner is aware of my collection, but not my connection with recovering the looted art. It is nought but a walk from the residences of the French delegation." Von Humboldt raised his eyebrows, cocking his head to the left.

"Are you suggesting Talleyrand is attempting to dispose of stolen artworks by selling them through private galleries?"

His companion shrugged. "I do not know, Major. I *do* think I wish to find it out, do you not?"

Henry poured more coffee, considering this news. "France has lost more than the wars. They have lost their allies as well as depleting their treasury. Offering looted treasures for sale would not be wise."

"The French are *not* wise," von Humboldt retorted. "Why else would they follow that absurd little man?"

"On this matter, baron, we will have to disagree," Henry responded without rancour. "As a people, the French are impulsive and quick to anger, but only a fool can claim Bonaparte has not been a formidable enemy. Europe may never be the same again."

Certainly, England will not. A heaviness fell over him as he remembered the men he commanded, many of whom would not be going home. Recalling the lady Rebecca's comments about his solitary life embedded Henry's grey feeling still deeper. As soon as the servers cleared their plates, he stood.

"I agree we need to look into it. Regardless of what they're about, we ought to know of it." A morning away from the perpetual negotiations of the congress was more than welcome. "It's a fine day for a ride unless you prefer a carriage?"

The baron shrugged again. "I do not keep one in Vienna. It is not because I cannot afford the equipage. I do not see the need. Vienna is so much the small city next to my Berlin."

Henry nodded his agreement. "Berlin is where I purchased my early Scharf. His lithographs are of some renown in London now."

"Scharf? Truly?" His friend sounded astonished as they awaited their horses. "I knew of him in Munich."

Henry sent his mount after the baron's. They had a pleasant morning ride, crossing the *Volksgarten* relatively uninterrupted. They dismounted beside the famous auction house where once again, Henry appeared to be one of the few Englishmen up and about this early, though the Viennese clearly stirred at cock's crow. Tethering his horse, Henry glanced idly into the Dorotheum window display— and stopped. He stood stock-still, staring at the newest work on show.

The painting showed off a typical woodland scene. A grove of trees. Two young children swinging on a naturally looped vine. It looked to be spring, and the bend of a river he thought he recognised. The children he *did* recognise—especially the older child, the boy with serious eyes squinting in the brightness of sunlight, as though he spent too much time indoors with his eyes focused on Latin or Greek. He was unlike the other child, the young girl with merry brown eyes and auburn curls. Her eyes were arresting—the deep, rich brown of fertile soil, shot through with a kind of blaze. Passion, substance, and a joy he'd seen in no girl's face since.

Henry stared, rooted to the spot like the oldest tree at Clayford, the one covered with epiphytes where he and his favourite playmate used to swing. Or rather, he allowed Louisa to sit in the thickest loop of vine, while he chivalrously did the swinging, watching her smile and her earthen eyes warm with laughter. He'd have done anything to make her laugh even then, though he'd been but fifteen years to her thirteen. There was something better in the world when Louisa smiled; something warmer when she laughed. He'd never forgotten the sound of Louisa's laugh. Like music, almost artistic, and as full of light as her fine landscapes.

"Major?" The baron's puzzled tone suggested he'd been speaking for some time. Henry had not heard a word.

Blinking himself out of reverie, he turned, unaccountably awkward. One did not stand motionless on a Viennese street, gaping at a painting like a youth on his first outing to the capital. He straightened his shoulders and looked about.

"I beg your pardon, baron." He coughed. "This work reminded me so forcibly of my home. It—erm—caught me unawares."

The baron nodded sympathetically. "Truly it is not easy to be billeted so far away and for so long a period."

"Indeed," Henry replied, unable to keep his gaze on his companion. Involuntarily, his head twisted, and he fixed his eyes on the painting once more. This time, he noticed the flower poised on the edge of a seemingly solid bough. *It can't be.* Henry shook himself and turned to his friend.

"How long is it since you were home?"

"A dozen or so years," the Prussian replied with a sigh. "I enjoy Vienna. Geneva before this. Paris before that, until Bonaparte, of course." He smiled with genuine delight. "This time, when I return to Berlin, I shall wed Rebecca there. Marriage—companionship—it is a state I find suits me better than I could have supposed. I cared for wedlock but little when I was a younger man like yourself, Major."

Henry laughed aloud. "There is not five years between us, baron."

"Is it so? Then you are late to the altar, my friend." The baron's moustaches quivered at his jest. "Rebecca believes every man ought to be in love. I am beginning to agree with her."

"Wedlock looks to agree with you, at any rate."

"But not with you, Major?" The baron made his statement into a question. "I saw your eyes light when they gazed upon this painting. You do not wear such a look when you dance at the balls of *Le Congrès.*"

"I was unaware my feelings showed so readily in my face," Henry muttered. Or perhaps the baron was a diplomat for a reason. Turning the subject appeared the least offensive course.

"This gallery is nearby?"

"A short walk." The baron accepted Henry's hint but shook his head. "Art is not life, my friend Major Musgrave. Remember this."

Henry followed the baron towards a narrow lane, glancing back at the painting. He already knew he'd be returning to the Dorotheum. There was a *reason* he remained unmarried.

The baron led him through a small doorway in single file. Henry looked around, noting that the establishment was well kept, though empty of other patrons. Several small rooms were lit from above by the high windows. Discreet signage offered instruction, and Henry muttered the translation under his breath: "These artworks are evenly spaced for exclusive viewing by appointment only." His friend was obviously as well connected in Vienna as he was in Berlin.

"Good afternoon, Baron von Humboldt." The owner of the *kunstgalerie* appeared before them, including them both in his bowing civilities.

"My friend Major Musgrave is a connoisseur as well as I," the baron explained. "May we view your portraits, Herr Christie?"

"Of course, of course, baron. All art lovers are welcome to a viewing. Step this way, gentlemen."

They followed Christie into an antechamber. Several portraits hung on the walls of the small room. Henry recognised the Vicomte DeVere, and another fine work showing a ravishing brunette artfully draped to resemble a goddess. He leaned closer to translate the description: *Evangeline Andrews as Venus, for the Vicomte DeVere.* Miss Andrews was DeVere's mistress and (it was rumoured) the mother of his ward. Henry studied the brushwork, noticing the delicate layering in the style of the Dutch school. It was a technique he admired.

"A fine work, is it not?" Herr Christie prompted.

"Very fine," Henry agreed. "What is its provenance?"

"A young Parisienne artist," Christie smiled again. "A student of Madame Vignée. His work is not widely known as yet. Does the major sense an opportunity?"

"What is the artist's name?"

"Traversant, sir. Louis Traversant. He is a genre painter certainly, but better known for his portraits."

"I can see why," Henry murmured, his gaze arrested by the vibrant image before him.

The baron led Henry to the largest exhibit in the chamber. "This is what I wished you to see, *mein freund.*"

"This is not a new work, Christie."

Herr Christie didn't reply, but Henry did not need him to describe the provenance. He recognised the artist's post-revolutionary style. *Vignée again.* So much more powerful than her earlier works. Henry recalled the rumours that Vignée had lost her entire family during The Terror, ironically inspiring some of her best pieces. He read the plaque to be certain he'd translated the title correctly: *Kassandra learns her fate.*

The woman in the portrait stared boldly out at the viewer, curvaceous and heavily busted. There was something unavoidably erotic about the way the draperies twisted about her as she realised her fate, knew she was destined to fall and fail. She held her head up regardless, looking him—looking *the viewer*, Henry worked to remind himself—in the eye without turning away.

Indeed, why should she? Kassandra's treatment at the hands of her own family had been shabby at best, her innocence stolen from her. Henry lifted his head to find the same astonishing eyes he'd noticed at the Dorotheum. Eyes he'd dreamed of...*Louisa's eyes.* Louisa, who'd stopped writing to him almost five months ago. She'd been bundled off, hidden, seemingly forgotten by her family and friends. *Not by me*, Henry vowed fiercely. How could anyone forget Louisa?

She had done all her father asked of her, except name her seducer—and for this, she was cast out. According to his godfather, Louisa claimed the man was too well connected. Henry had no difficulty believing it. Still, he tried to find the bastard. His rage remained unspent, but he'd not forgotten. He would not leave this earth without satisfaction on Louisa's behalf. Of this, he was equally certain.

Henry realised he'd been staring into Kassandra's eyes far longer than seemed appropriate. There was something about their expression: a fear matched with defiance that he found undeniably alluring. Louisa always reminded him of Kassandra, the seeress destined never to be believed. A tragic figure and a fit subject for a neo-classicist like Vignée. Henry's eyes followed the girl's tightly muscled calves, her firm thighs artfully twined with silks—and was that *blood* running down her thighs? He'd not noticed such a detail before. Were his eyes playing tricks? He leaned closer, drawing back as someone behind him uttered a discreet sound. Glancing over his shoulder, he saw Christie watching him.

"Do you wish to offer for the Vignée, Major?"

Henry smiled ruefully. "Another time, perhaps." He signalled to the baron with his eyes and they exited, walking rapidly back to their horses.

"It is not one of the stolen works, baron," Henry declared flatly. "It is, however, a later Vignée. Genuine, unless I miss my guess."

The baron sighed. "I beg your pardon, Major. I did not intend to waste your morning."

Henry smiled. "You did no such thing. I am grateful for the opportunity to examine her *Kassandra* so closely."

"Almost too closely," von Humboldt winked at him. "*Herr* Christie behaves like a jealous lover around his collection."

Henry laughed. "Art is a mistress for men like Christie. Expensive, colourful, and of course, beautiful."

His friend laughed with him. "This is very apt, Major. For Christie, and for you as well, I am thinking."

"Perhaps," Henry replied, distracted again as they reached the Dorotheum. "I'm going in there," he jerked his head toward the bay window.

"This does not surprise me," his Prussian friend replied. "I ought to tell you that I have already offered for the woodland scene."

"Have you indeed?" Henry tried to smile, but he could not do it. Not this time.

"I see I am already outbid," von Humboldt uttered a regretful sigh.

Something tightened in Henry's chest. If the painting was what he thought it was...*Louisa*. He'd find the funds, even if he had to sell his entire private collection. He squared his shoulders, glancing between the baron and the artwork as if he expected the painting to somehow disappear, like the Roman art denied by Talleyrand.

"I shall meet you back at the congress, Major. We lunch with the French again at noon." The Prussian inclined his head and smiled. "I wish you luck at the Dorotheum. They are ruthless."

"I'm sure." Henry entered the great auction house as though readying for battle. The walls and pedestals were replete with beautiful works: sculptures, clocks, tapestries, even tea sets, but none of this registered beyond a gleam of colour or the curve of an elegant carving. His heart raced as though he'd fallen prey to ague and his palms—his *palms* of all things—were damp. Swallowing nothing in an attempt to steady his pulse, Henry stilled his shaking hands with an effort. He'd faced a thousand Frenchmen in battle and ridden unflinchingly into cannon fire. Surely, he might experience less trepidation in approaching a man about a painting? *A painting depicting an incident known only to myself—and Louisa.*

Chapter 4

"At your service, Major Musgrave." The auctioneer introduced himself with a bow.

Henry indicated the painting. "The work in the window—"

"Ah, yes." The auctioneer smiled. "A departure from the artist's other works, you know."

"Oh?" Henry feigned disinterest. A tingling sensation made its way along the back of his neck, like an itch.

"Traversant is the artist of the moment in Paris. His prices will, of course, increase on his admission to The Paris Academy."

"His admission is imminent?"

"So say the rumours," the auctioneer replied. "He is better known for his portraits and his nudes," the guide continued. "Would you care to examine them?"

"I should be most interested." Henry maintained his appearance of polite indifference. "The work in the window?" he pressed.

"*Camarades* is one of his earliest pieces," the man replied.

"The title translates as *Comrades*," Henry mused. "It does not look like the French countryside. Could it be English?"

The fellow shrugged. "I never heard Traversant was in England. There are oaks and elms enough in *Ile-de-France*, Major."

Henry gazed again at the painting. The feeling at the back of his neck intensified. Repressing an awkward shiver, he wondered at his inability to manage sensation today. "Do you meet the artists yourself?"

The auctioneer shook his head. "I have a man in France for that sort of thing, excellent fellow. He kept his head so far as I know and sends the works here, escorted by coach." The businessman paused, fixing Henry with a shrewd stare. "I've had several offers for this one, you know. Upwards of twelve gulden. Would you care to make a purchase today?"

Henry smiled, hoping his enthusiasm did not show so plainly on his face. "Perhaps. When is your auction?"

The auctioneer handed him a catalogue. "Three days after Christmastide, sir, if I do not dispose of the piece prior."

I'll be there. Henry pocketed the paperwork. "You mentioned portraits?" It seemed important to learn all he could about this Traversant fellow. For reasons he could not explain, he held his breath as he followed the man to the rear *anzeigeraum.* This was the space for showcasing major pieces for the upcoming auction. The largest canvas marked a point of difference from the half dozen or so portraits gracing the other walls. Placed in the centre of the room in a beam of light, it drew the eye.

The painting depicted a female nude, beautifully curvaceous, her hand slipping suggestively beneath a draped cloth. *It can't be.* Henry found his eye seeking the face of the buxom lady captured in what appeared to be the act of arousing herself in pleasure. He uttered a sigh of disappointment when he saw the girl's face turned determinedly away, as if she were gazing into the canvas, away from the voyeur whose eyes fell irresistibly to her perfectly formed derriere.

It was as though he watched her through a keyhole, presented only with her curls, her back, and the curve of her disappearing breast as she faced away from her viewer. Henry wanted to reach for her shoulder, turn her back to him, take her clearly erect nipple between his teeth…

"It's extraordinary," he said aloud, because it seemed the auctioneer waited out his silence for so long that Henry was required to say *something.*

"Isn't it?" The guide looked smug. "His Grace himself has requested a viewing."

"Wellington? I've no doubt." Henry raised a brow. The Duke would enjoy such a spectacle as much as his public would condemn him for it. "Will the viewing be held here?"

"It is hardly the sort of artwork we'd exhibit in a public salon," the guide commented.

Henry hardly heard him, his eyes trailing the curve of one raised leg, tempting the viewer to a glimpse of inner thigh barely hidden behind the tiniest scrap of billowing silk. He leaned closer—*was* it silk? Why did this matter? He caught his breath at the mark on her thigh. A birthmark? *A butterfly. It can't be.* Unthinking, he reached out a hand.

A soft clearing of a throat admonished him—again—and Henry stepped back, running his eye repeatedly over the woman's form, somehow managing to tangle it all up among her tumbled auburn curls, which fell ... well, they fell in a distinct wave that reminded him, that reminded him—*oh dear God, I have to get out of here.*

Or at least face a wall, like the artist's painted subject.

Was this exhibit intentionally libidinous? The Dorotheum was not the sort of place one expected to find—Henry glanced sideways at his host. The auctioneer fixed his gaze upon the work with rapt attention, his eyes following the lines of the womanly form on display. Oh, the man knew all right. Whether the artist intended to titillate his viewers or not, there wasn't a doubt in Henry's mind that the exhibitors intended their placement to have this effect.

"What is the title?" he asked, to break a hush that seemed too charged for polite conversation.

"*Une femme astucieuse,*" came the response.

"*The artful woman.* Clever," he commented.

"For a Frenchman." The auctioneer seemed to feel this was required. "It's the Traversant piece I've had the most interest in. The story goes that the model is his mistress."

"Aren't they all?" Henry replied.

"Would you care to offer for this one?" his guide asked again.

Henry shook his head with a smile he hoped hid his disappointment. "If His Grace is interested, you'll not find too many who'd care to trump his offer," he pointed out, drawing his card case from his waistcoat. "If he does not purchase, you may find me at Wimpole House."

The auctioneer smiled and bowed. "You're welcome anytime, sir. It's been a privilege."

Henry bowed and took his leave. Once outside, he paused before *Camarades* again, unable to prevent himself from staring. He'd no idea how this Traversant fellow managed to paint images of events to which he could not possibly be privy, but he was determined to discover him.

Later. Right now, he'd best hurry to his luncheon with Talleyrand's envoys. Should this meet prove successful, it may release him from his evening engagements. Henry sighed. A night of brandy and books beside the fireplace tempted him more than another card party. He smiled faintly as he imagined Louisa's response to such a desire.

"Why, Henry," she'd said one time, when he'd requested silence while he completed his studies. "Have you not heard that children who read too much grow up weakened? How will you make a soldier now?" Her teasing smile made it impossible for him to be offended, as did those eyes of hers, lit with some inner flame. He shook his head, nudging his horse gently forwards. The streets of Vienna grew busy and he'd no wish to be caught behind a dust cart.

***

In the end, Talleyrand's men were no more forthcoming over luncheon than they'd been the previous evening. By the time Henry had written his latest report, another long night of smiles and souse lay behind him. He ignored his books, taking himself off to bed with another large brandy.

The girl drags him, gasping and spluttering, through the strongest current to the sandy slope where she hauls him up, he knows not how. His eyes flicker open, uncertain of life for the first time, his heart's rhythm similarly erratic—and her smile of relief becomes a laugh, an embrace, a heartfelt kiss. The press of her warm pink lips against his cheek, turning his head, meeting her mouth with his own charged, unexpected—wholly impassioned and unexpected—response as his hand slides against her smooth thigh, the one with the butterfly. She kisses him fervently, clumsily, before pushing him tenderly away. He smiles down at her soaked chemise, clinging, revealing in bare outline everything he wishes to know about girls in that moment.

Henry sat bolt upright, the surreal taste of her on his lips. He was startled to discover he was bathed in sweat, heart racing as though he were pursued. Or in love. Shaking his head hard, he aimed to dispel the dream from his mind. *A dream?* It was more memory than dream. He shook his head again, blinking into returning consciousness. It *was* a memory. The sheer terror as he hurtled down toward the stream. The precise shiver of his skin as he hit river water, chill from the recent thaw. The shock of the cold, the fear of the water—he couldn't swim, never learned, and the current was strong. He remembered Louisa's shout and a word he'd never known any young lady to utter aloud.

Obviously, he'd taken a dunking, but afterwards—Henry smiled as he recollected his first kiss. The kiss that saved his life. He'd left for Cambridge the next day.

A sharp tap at his door was followed by Baker's tousled head and his arm holding a small candelabrum. "I beg your pardon, Major. I'd not expected to find you—"

"Awake?" Henry suggested, glancing toward the drapes. There was no sign of light. "What is it?"

"The General, sir. Your godfather."

Henry rose and began to dress. "A message?"

"An appearance."

Henry gaped at his aide. "Uncle George is *here*? Gracious, man, next time, begin with that." He could not truly be angry. Baker had been unceremoniously disturbed as much as himself. "Never mind. Inform him I shall attend him directly—and alert von Humboldt's butler. It's no easy journey from the Embassy."

"Shall I request the baron?"

Henry shook his head. "Let the man sleep. If it's Crown business, he cannot be present." Reaching for his scarlet jacket, he pulled the collar into place as best he could.

"I've lit a fire in the morning room. He awaits you there."

"All right, Baker." Henry finished his buttons and commandeered the candelabrum as they moved into the hall. "See if you can knock the old fellow up some food."

"Very good, sir." His man lit a candle stub before descending the back stairs.

What urgency brought the General to Vienna at such a time? News about the missing artworks? *Or about Louisa?* Henry's dream came back to him, and he paused a moment outside the morning room door. Best to smooth all trace of such memories from his face before meeting Louisa's father. The grandfather clock stood sentry by the door, reading two am: *morning room indeed*. Taking a breath, Henry turned the handle.

"Good morning, godfather." He bowed.

The General rose immediately, bowing in response. "Forgive my intrusion, Henry. I desire to consult you on a matter of urgency."

"I am sure my host is happy to see you at any time, sir, as am I. I hope, however, you have not distressed yourself by journeying in haste. A letter would not serve?"

"It is too delicate a matter for correspondence. Besides, the continental post is unreliable." The great commander passed a shuddering hand over his face.

Henry could not imagine his godfather's delicacy overset by matters of state, no matter how precarious the politics. *So this is about Louisa.* He studied the man before him. Uncle George seemed to have aged precipitously in the past few months. The wars were reason enough, but Henry knew the depths of the man's affection for his daughter. Since Louisa's disappearance the General's stoic demeanour had begun to exhibit signs of wear. Pouring out two large brandies, he handed one to his godfather and took a seat. The General preferred to pace, drink in hand, until he stopped, swallowed a large gulp of liquor, and met Henry's gaze.

"Have you heard from Louisa?"

"I've not, General," Henry replied. "I have written to her at Cologne, as you requested." He neglected to add that he'd written more than once. In truth, he'd written regularly, though he had no clear idea of her household. Louisa always expressed joy in hearing from him. *Used to,* he reminded himself. *Louisa used to express joy in our correspondence.* She also used to reply promptly.

If his maths was accurate, her child ought to have been born by now and fostered out. Why then, had Louisa not returned to Clayford House? Why had she not replied to any of her family? To *him*? Henry could not shake the feeling that something was amiss with his friend. *Friend?* He shrugged inwardly, trying to hide his irritation.

The General refilled both glasses too generously for this hour. "I've heard nothing," he said in gruff tones.

"You received no notice of anything amiss during her confinement?"

The General shook his head and shivered, as though all mention of Louisa's condition pained him physically.

"Have you seen responses to your letters?" the General persisted.

"Nothing in the positive, General. There is a war on, or rather there was, and France remains unstable, but—" He paused, the weight of expectation pressing, unease filling the room, as though the General had mixed their snifters with fear instead of water. "What is it you know?"

"All my letters are returned unopened." His godfather did not sound surprised. "I've heard, through a friend, that my daughter no longer occupies the Cologne residence I established when her—condition—became obvious.

"On receipt of this news, I sent out inquiries and booked passage on the first available packet," the General continued. "An express arrived here as I did." He held out an embossed vellum, doing his best to obscure the avian crest with his thumb, but Henry saw it: one of the noble houses of Prussia. His gut tightened as he digested this.

It was not for him to criticise his godfather, but to send his daughter among strangers, at such a time, without even her maid...Louisa, alone and pregnant, in a strange country among people who did not know her at all—*and who have, apparently, lost sight of her.*

Henry felt himself coming perilously close to insubordination. He took up his glass alongside the document. Whatever news was forthcoming would most assuredly require a drink. Fear mingled with fury in his breast as he read:

1 December 1814
Rue de Seine
Paris

Dear General,

Per your request, I endeavour to find why your letters receive no response. First of all, accept my assurance that they have most certainly been received. I have today received responses to many careful inquiries but have no good news.

The young woman you seek is no longer resident in Cologne. I am told she left under the protection of a young artist about whom little is known (except to declare him reliable, I cannot name any source, and I beg you will not inquire).

The artist is said to be Louis Traversant. This may be affectation as no artist of that name registers at l'Académie. Rumour has him residing in le Louvre apartments, where many libertine pleasures find indulgence.

I have not seen the lady myself. However, I am informed she matches your description and the miniature you were good enough to send me. Regarding Traversant, I have made as discreet inquiry as I am able. Beyond knowing that his work sells both in Prussia and in what remains of the French empire, I have learned nothing. I have met no one who meets him personally.

I shall write when I know more, though deeper inquiry may absolve discretion. This, I know, you are desirous to avoid.

Your sincere friend, at your service, as always,
W

Henry had faced enemies in wartime and battled personally with a range of adversaries, but not once had he felt anything like the killing rage that rose within him now. He swore viciously and far too loudly, crumpling the letter into a misshapen pile before tossing it into the fire.

He looked toward his godfather. "I beg your pardon, sir."

The General hardly seemed to notice, staring at his brandy as though it might speak his daughter's whereabouts. Henry stood by the fireplace, gazing into the flames. He did not need to dissemble, nor could he pretend to misunderstand. Louisa must truly be desperate to countenance becoming mistress to an artist—and an unknown one at that. Seduced and deserted, left with child by a man she was too frightened to expose. A man who could not be impossible to trace were it not for the protection of a powerful duke.

So far Louisa's situation had not reached the ears of the ton. Henry eyed his godfather. Was the duke blackmailing the General? Higher-ranked officials than Uncle George had been put to worse use by the Duke of Carston. The duke was no fighter; of this Henry was certain. He was equally certain he could compel His Grace to reveal the name of Louisa's seducer—but what future could Louisa have with such a coward, even if Henry and the General forced him to the altar rails?

Sweet, lovely Louisa deserved better. She deserved a man who loved her, appreciated her. Much as Henry wished to meet the blackguard by appointment, he was none too sorry for this chance to preserve Louisa from such a union. *So she may become a Frenchman's mistress?* He felt sick to his stomach.

"You've heard I'm for Paris at sunrise?" he glanced towards the window.

"Hence my haste," came the reply. "I wish to request your aid, if...if..." The General's courage seemed to fail him.

"Any news of her whereabouts and I am at your disposal," Henry offered and then, because he could not help saying so, "I believe your informant is correct. Louisa may be in France, and with Traversant."

His words hardly seemed to register with the General. His godfather faced him, his brow furrowed with tension. "This must go no further, Henry."

"I understand, sir. While my immediate desire is to locate this Frenchman and serve him as he deserves, you need have no fear that my anger—which is very great in this moment—will overcome my discretion." Henry inhaled heavily, swallowing his rage. "Did your friend happen to learn of your daughter's health? Is Louisa recovered?"

"There are reports she is in health, and I thank you," Beresford murmured. "I oughtn't to have sent her away." The older man seemed measurably greyer as he shook his head in self-reproach. "It is fitting that she writes you. I do not wish to pry into your affairs, Henry, but—" the General hesitated. "Forgive me—she still refuses to say whom?"

"Not a word." Henry's tone spoke resignation as well as anger. "Is there no one in the whole of England prepared to gainsay the Duke of Carston?"

"No one to whom we may apply," his godfather replied. "A fact of which His Grace is assuredly aware."

"This is not her doing, sir. It is *not*," Henry burst out, closing his eyes as his godfather's despair bore heavily upon him.

"To whose influence do you impute it?" The flatness of the General's tone showed his ire only to one who knew him as well as Henry did.

"I cannot blame you for doing as you have done, sir."

The General shrugged. There was something else. Henry could feel it. Tension gathered in the room, like clouds before a lightning strike. *Perhaps I ought to duck?*

"I ought not to have sent her away," his godfather repeated. "She deserved—*deserves*—better from me, from all the family. And now—" The great man's voice shuddered to a halt.

"What is it, General?" Henry prompted.

"There are rumours that France remains unsafe."

Henry shrugged. "Bonaparte is secure. The Republic is dead, and there are always rumours."

Firm lips shook as the General delivered his next piece of news. "I have intelligence of advanced plans to aid Bonaparte's escape."

"*Escape?*" Henry whispered, shock seeping slowly through him. He sank into the nearest chair, feeling as weary as the General was wont to look. "Then—the wars are *not* over?" He could not care that his words sounded like a plea. He so badly did not want this news to be true.

"I had it from a fellow aboard *The Inconstant*. A more aptly named vessel you could not find." The General's barked laugh bore no resemblance to humour.

"How likely is such an event, and what might he do?"

The General shrugged. "What else? If he is successful, he will march on Paris—and we must return to war."

"Return to war," Henry echoed, then shot to his feet. "If these rumours prove true, is it at all certain the Paris Academy reopens?"

"Nothing is certain concerning France at the moment." His godfather's defeated tone was so unlike the commander who'd directed battalions that Henry feared for the man's health. If Traversant did not return to Paris, Louisa could be anywhere, in which case...*in which case, she is truly lost to me.*

It did not bear thinking about. He remained standing, staring into his empty glass. He wasn't one for heavy drinking, but he was sorely tempted this night.

A moment later, the General seized his arm. "Go while you can, Henry. Bring her home. Bring Louisa home. If she is caught up in this," the General's fists curled, but his booming voice fell to a desperate whisper, "I shan't forgive myself if she is somehow caught up in this. Injured because of my—" He could not finish, extending his shaking hands in a plea towards Henry's own.

"We have a direction," Henry replied firmly, clasping his godfather's palm. "If Louisa has removed to Paris, I shall find her."

"This is exactly as I wish it." His godfather clutched his drink, seating himself at last. "And if she has become a—" He gulped.

Henry closed his eyes briefly, giving the older man a moment to master himself.

"If she is living under this Traversant's protection, I will find him out." He bit back further speech, slowly and deliberately unclenching his fist. "Such news need not be known in London."

The General nodded, gripping Henry's hand so hard he hoped he may still be able to grasp a quill. His godfather released him and took up his partly filled glass. Topping it to the brim, he raised it to Henry in an ironic toast.

"To deserving better."

Clinking his crystal against Henry's, he downed the contents in a single swallow.

"Deserving better," Henry echoed.

Just as Louisa does.

Chapter 5

"You ought not to go among decent people," the lacemaker spat as Louisa passed the old woman. Holding tight to Henri, Louisa returned to her studio, leaving her errands undone. She needed materials, not to mention bread and fruit, but the rumours about "Traversant and *la mademoiselle*" were an unwelcome distraction. Besides, she did not regret her son. *Not for a moment.* Sighing, she shrugged off the heaviness such cruelties left in their wake, returning to her art.

Taking up a floral prop, she positioned herself opposite the mirror. Adjusting the garland at her temple, she eyed the result critically. *Too much for Psyche?* Louisa grimaced at her reflection. A true goddess would be crowned with real, vibrant, living flowers adorning her brow. Not wilted, day-old ones borrowed from Madame Vignée's extensive array of gifted bouquets.

"It's a good thing your mama has an imagination, as well as a commission, Henri." She checked on her slumbering infant before returning to the clay model of Canova's famous sculpture. Running her hands over the lines of Cupid hovering over his sleeping Psyche, Louisa moved across to her divan, attempting to imitate the pose of the love god's mate. She stretched herself out before the mirror, naked but for her flowers. The lines of Psyche's body were not as challenging as those of the winged god, suspended in the air above his lover. How she was going to paint such a vision she did not yet know, but she could make a beginning at least. She estimated she had two hours if nothing disturbed Henri.

A moment later, a series of loud bangs shocked her from her stool. Racing across the studio, she barely donned her linen in time as her art tutor threw open the door, rushing in with all the energy of a storm wind.

"Ah, *ma chère amie*, you are here—*bon*." Madame Vignèe paused as she took in Louisa's unfortunate state. "You must dress, Louisa. They will be here any moment to demand the departure."

Her teacher's breathlessness was contagious. Louisa hurried to complete her toilette, Madame Vignèe stepping in to bind her breasts before Louisa gathered wits enough to ask for details.

"Who will be here, Madame, and why must we leave?"

"*I*," her harried companion corrected. "It is I who must leave, *mon amie*. You may remain here. I cannot."

"For Heaven's sake, why?" Louisa persisted. Madame's behaviour often raised eyebrows, but she was an artist. Her scandals were tame compared to much of what went on at *le Louvre*.

"I–I have been expelled from *l'Académie*," Madame Vignée announced.

"Gracious, why?" Louisa froze in the act of capping her hair.

"It is my *Madone et enfant*," she sighed gustily, sketches of Louisa's nudes floating off an end table to land at her feet.

"The *Madonna and Child* for which I posed with Henri?"

"*Oui*," Madame answered. "My Madonna is '*scandaleux*,' they say. A redhead, like *Marie-Madeleine*. She smiles with *teeth*, they say. I cannot help this. I paint her true to life and my model, she is the firebrand." She shrugged at Louisa. "Your smile, Louisa. Your—*clivage*. They say it is 'too real.'"

Louisa's auburn brows rose and she did her best to hide a smile. "This is because they *are* real," she replied, offended on her friend's behalf. "And don't you mean *mes seins*?"

Madame Vignèe threw a hand over her round mouth in a mockery of shock. "If your Englishman could zee you now..." She wagged her head meaningfully.

Louisa's face fell. "Madame," she warned. "There is no Englishman."

Her friend rolled her eyes the way Louisa had only ever seen French artists manage. "Now it is *you* who are being English." The older woman tutted in her throat. "I have had three husbands and some dozens of lovers, my dear Louisa. I know a woman's heart when I see it. Do not attempt to prevaricate—" Madame's command of English seemed to evolve as Louisa opened her lips to object.

"Not in my studio if you please. We will have only raw honesty *here*," her tutor commanded.

"Is this why I must continue as Traversant?" Louisa asked, repressing a shiver.

"You know you must. *L'Académie* only admits four women a year, and their quota is filled. If you are to be admitted, it must be as Traversant." Madame shot a glance at the cradle. "We cannot wait, *mon amie*. You have expenses too *immédiatement*, do you not?"

Louisa blushed, nodding. "I do not like the subterfuge," she acknowledged, but Madame's logic was irrefutable.

When her teacher's voice came again, Louisa heard its softness and the great fondness Madame had for herself and her son. "I do not judge you, my Louisa," she replied. "Only those who abandon you. However, they sent you to me. You and Henri." She sighed as she gazed at the child. "I can be grateful to your *père* for this."

Madame must be thinking of her own lost little children. One stillborn, the other dead of illness during The Terror. "It was after I lost my own Henri that you found me in Cologne, like a miracle. Burgeoning with new life, you were, like Paris, like the Madonna herself."

"If you mean to remind me that I was as round as a cannonball and almost destitute, I remember it well," Louisa replied drily, recalling her first month alone in Cologne. She'd been fortunate to find work with Madame. Fortunate to have her talent noticed, encouraged, nurtured. She considered herself most blessed of all to have gained this woman's friendship.

Madame's steadfast encouragement reminded Louisa of Henry, who'd been the first friend to encourage her art. If Madame was her inspiration, Louisa's memories of Henry felt like anchorage. Her childhood friend's enlistment was the only selfish act of which Louisa could accuse him. Dear Henry was that rarest of military officers—a profoundly good man.

He was also the model in her mind's eye for Traversant, whose existence owed as much to Madame's wits as to Louisa's. Placing a miniature she'd created of her alter ego into her friend's hands, Louisa smiled. "A small gift, Madame, hardly adequate to repay your kindness."

The older woman laughed at the fictional persona. "This is fine work, Louisa. You will reveal yourself as soon as you are able. Next year, perhaps. Meanwhile, Traversant will be admitted to *l'Académie* for this Christmas." Madame returned to practicalities. "Your submission is *superbe*." She kissed the air with her fingers.

"You have not yet seen it, Madame," Louisa protested, clamping down on a surge of pride.

"Do I need to see it? I do not. You are the finest artist to submit this year. You have had the advantage of the finest tutor." Here she bowed rather than curtsied, answering Louisa's bemused look.

"You may doubt your art, mademoiselle, but do not doubt my judgment. False modesty is a waste of paint. I insist my studio remain an honest place. Real lives, real lovers, and real *seins*, whatever those stuffy old men at *l'Académie* may say. Now, hurry and dress. They come too soon to expose me and cast me out." She lifted a white arm over her eyes as if to shield herself from an oncoming attack.

Louisa completed pinning her hair before the giant mirror. "If they do not want you, they cannot have me either," she declared.

Madame tutted again. "Do not be foolish, my dear. This is Henri's home now. You will stay here as Traversant and receive my stipend."

"Where will you go, Madame?"

Her friend winked. "My lover has a home of his own in Montmartre. We leave Paris as soon as he can procure us a horse. He is a vicomte—did I not say?" She curtsied this time, beaming at Louisa then clapping her hands together. "I have arranged it all splendidly, have I not?"

Louisa completed her male costume, donning her false goatee and moustaches. Taking a deep breath, she presented herself to Madame for inspection, feeling both brave and foolish. Courage was a required ingredient of art, one that cost far more than grapes.

"*Bon*," Madame declared. "Should they invite you to a tavern, remember not to drink ale. The glue of your moustaches will not hold if you do."

"I am aware," Louisa smiled, "and I am not inclined to ale, Madame." She executed a very proper bow (holding an image of Henry Musgrave firmly in her mind) and turned to respond to the loud banging on the other side of their apartment door. Deepening her voice in imitation of Henry again, Louisa stepped into the hallway to address the "stuffy old men" in impeccable French.

"*Bonjour*, gentlemen, may I inquire as to the cause of this disturbance?"

"We wish to speak with your teacher, Traversant," said one, a Bohemian who'd not produced anything but critique since the emperor's arrest.

"She is no longer available at this address," Louisa replied, closing the door firmly behind her. *Dear God, can they not speak lower? If Henri should wake, I shall lose an hour's work.*

"Ah!" replied the second gentleman, lifting his fat hands into the air. "Excellent, *monsieur*. You have expelled her as well. Well done."

"I have done no such thing," Louisa replied. "Her patron, the vicomte, has commissioned a study of his estate. Madame Vignée is en route to his residence. You will find her there." She paused. "I must return to my work. Interruptions are un-welcome at this time. The light, you know."

"Indeed," replied the third gentleman, an impeccably garbed Parisienne without exhibits this year. "The light, the light is perfect this evening."

"It is," Louisa replied, preparing to slip back inside.

"Did you receive my message, Traversant?" the third traditionalist asked.

Louisa turned back to him. "*Non*, monsieur."

"Two gentlemen visited *Le Salon* today. From *le Congrès de Vienne*. The pair spent much time looking over our exhibits." The three men shared smirks of self-congratulation. "One of them requested for you most particularly."

Louisa stared at the third academician. "For me? You're certain?"

The man shrugged. "I told him we have many works by *established* members of the Academy. Nevertheless, he requested your presence at Véfour's for six this evening."

"Gracious." Louisa barely remembered to lower her voice. Clearing her throat, she nodded, looking the man in the eye. *Only women stare at their feet.*

"He has a commission, I believe. From Vienna," one of the other men added, staring back at her, clearly awaiting clarification.

"The Dorotheum accepted some of my early works for sale," Louisa explained. "They likely referred him on." She took a breath.

"I thank you, sir. I shall attend Véfour's this evening and await his arrival."

"And we shall await your submission to *l'Académie*," the other replied. "To gain international commissions before you are even registered is no small achievement, Traversant. *Félicitations*."

Louisa bowed (again, picturing Henry), speculating whether these gentlemen would be so hearty in their praise if they knew she leaked milk beneath her linen. "The light," she repeated, turning back to her apartments, heart beating like one of Bonaparte's batteurs.

A commission from Vienna? Perhaps Henri's first Christmas need not be so lean after all. Slipping back towards safety, she met Madame's gleeful face with a smile. "Did you hear, Madame?"

"I did." She embraced Louisa tightly.

"My strappings," Louisa gasped.

"Of course." Madame stood back. "At least you will eat well tonight. The fare at Véfour's is said to be *magnifique*." She kissed her fingers in the air again.

"But I cannot attend, Madame." Louisa's delight faded. "I cannot hope to pass as Traversant for an entire meal, nor to avoid wine. What sort of agent will believe in an artist who will not accept drinks?"

Madame acknowledged this point with a tweak of her head.

"Besides, you know Henri is not yet weaned," Louisa finished.

Madame shrugged. "Then it is I who shall dine divinely, *mon amie*. I will negotiate the commission for you, if you will trust me to do this?"

"*Oui*, Madame, of course I trust you." Louisa hesitated. "You must take a fee, of course."

"I shall take a fee," Madame agreed. "Five percent. Is it a contract?"

Louisa snorted. "You know perfectly well that the proper fee for an artistic agent is thirty percent, Madame, and I am not an established artist. Why, I do not have registration at *l'Académie* as yet."

"Always you make *les objections, mon amie*." She gazed seriously at Louisa. "You must learn a little better. I am not a registered agent so I command less. If you insist, I will accept fifteen percent. You will only be paying over to me for tutelage, in any case," she added shrewdly.

Louisa laughed at the truth of this. "I thank you, Madame. I am most grateful to you, always."

Chapter 6

Henry had not been long in Paris and he didn't intend to stay past Christmas. His French was dreadful for a start. Von Humboldt's expertise in this area more than compensated for his penchant for early morning rides. Studying the baroque facade of the buildings as they made their way back to their lodgings, he sighed in time with his friend.

"Do you find Paris much changed, baron?"

"Indeed," replied his friend. "Last time I visited there was no sovereign, no salon to attend, and *le Louvre* open to all."

"Only a few days a week, I gather."

The Prussian shrugged. "All great art requires time to create, as well as to exhibit, Major. Did you not find this yourself when you created your works?"

Henry laughed. "You are mistaken, baron, if you believe my unripe daubings ever merited such an appellation. My childhood acquaintance, on the other hand, produced work of significant distinction. Nothing hastened my military ambitions so much as knowing I could never achieve work as fine."

"This is the friend whose interrupted correspondence has concerned you for his well-being?"

"*Her* well-being," Henry corrected automatically, wishing he hadn't. The fewer people who knew of Louisa's circumstances, the safer she would be.

"A lady painter." The baron's interest sharpened noticeably. "How unique."

Henry's cheeks warmed as he felt the baron's eyes on him. His friend ventured nothing further, but he found himself the subject of the Prussian's acute focus as they travelled the Tuileries Garden boundary.

"Do you hear anything further regarding *Le Salon de Noël*? There are enough rumours about the new young artist setting the Paris Salon on its ear." The baron's turn of subject mended little.

"Rumours, but very little fact, baron. Traversant is something of a mystery, it seems," Henry replied, flexing his shoulder. "Unlike most of the artists keen to make a name for themselves, he rarely attends the Salon."

"This is unusual," von Humboldt agreed. "If the price fetched is of no meaning to the painter, then collectors such as you or I have little with which to bargain. Do you intend to seek him at his studio?"

"If I must." Henry turned into the courtyard of the Hôtel Westminster and dismounted, avoiding the shrewd gaze of the baron. "I am in hopes he will accept our invitation to dine this evening."

"You may be in luck there, Major, given our friends at *l'Académie* indicate he has no patron."

Henry accompanied his friend indoors. "I hope your surmise is correct." *Though accosting the rake at his studio offers more opportunity for satisfaction than dining out in Paris.* He could hardly call Traversant out in public—not if he intended to protect Louisa.

The concierge stepped forward to take their capes and gloves. Henry signalled that they'd like a drink. Following the baron's example and holding his numb hands out towards the hall fireplace, he eyed the clock.

"We've not long before we must dress."

"I shall dine here at *le hôtel*," the baron declared with a little shrug.

"You do not wish to join us?" Henry looked at the Prussian in surprise, unease twinging through him.

"I wish for nothing better, *mein freund*. However, when a gentleman pursues a lady, it is best he proceed without intrusion, is it not?"

"I did not refer to any ladies," protested Henry, stepping back from the flames. His face was warm enough, thank you.

The baron spoke in an undertone. "You mentioned your artistic acquaintance. A collector does not need to meet with an artist to gain his work, especially when you may purchase any of a dozen paintings at *Le Salon de Noël*. I can only assume it is not Traversant's art you seek."

Henry opened his mouth, closed it again, then met his friend's gaze. "Very well, baron, I *do* seek my friend. It is not like her to disrupt our correspondence in this manner." He blinked once. "More than this, I cannot divulge." Considering his last unanswered letter and the exposed feelings it contained, he squared his shoulders and held his ground—but he had to know. "What gave me away?"

"Your voice when you speak of her—regret and longing. The lover's instinct to protect. The way you speak of Traversant, and your interrogations of the men at *l'Académie*. I'd no idea you could be so intimidating when discussing art, Major. This day has been quite the revelation." He accepted his drink and watched the server depart before he continued.

"There is a connection between your lady painter and Traversant, I am guessing. I am also aware you had a late-night visitor before we left Vienna." The Prussian flung up a palm as Henry opened his mouth to speak. "Pray, do not elaborate. I do not require details, but the Frenchman can interest you for no other reason."

The baron smiled and held out his hand. "There is no offense with me, I hope?"

Henry shook his hand. "Not at all, baron. The matter is delicate, and I appreciate your discretion. Forgive me in your turn." He decided then and there never to play his friend at any card table.

"There is nothing to forgive," the baron replied. "I wish you success in your outing this evening. I shall enjoy my beer and dine with an acquaintance who may reveal something more regarding the missing horses of Saint Mark."

"Then may your evening be as successful as my own." Henry bowed as he headed to their double-bedded room to dress. As he ascended the stairs, he caught sight of another work he'd been tasked with returning to the allies. His visit to Paris had at least a credible disguise.

As long as his astute friend did not penetrate the truth of Louisa's circumstances as he'd so neatly dissected Henry's desires. *Next time, I'll come alone*, he vowed before finishing his evening dress. There would not be a next time, he reminded himself. He must do his duty, and he must protect Louisa. Everything paled beside those two objectives, even art. He kept a close eye on the clock as he donned his caped coat and hurried to his venue. Arriving before Traversant seemed the best course. While regaining Louisa was not precisely a military exercise, a sound strategy could do him no harm. Besides, the more Henry considered his service record, the less likely he was to forget himself and do something rash—like call the blackguard out.

He sat at the back table of Véfour's, visually dividing the room into quadrants. Scanning the back of each male head, he'd wager he might know Traversant on sight. The description from the men at the Academy had hardly been distinguished. The "gentleman artist" he sought was "red-haired, slight, wore woven maroon, a large hat always," and owned "zee small moustaches." Henry hoped slim young men were not numerous this evening and thought askance of artists who seemed to notice so little in the way of detail. He'd also been warned Traversant did not drink, which he'd assumed was a relativism. What this might indicate, Henry could not guess.

A whisper rustled through the restaurant. Like the other diners, Henry turned to see who had disturbed the elegance of *poulet fricassee* and fine red wine, cellared (no doubt) prior to the revolution that had proved so deadly to good food as well as great art. He stood automatically as he recognised the entrance of Madame Vignée. His astonishment grew as she made her way towards his side of the dining room, only to curtsey before him.

"Good evening." She spoke in heavily accented English, with confident manners that were not overbearing. She was several years older than him, but she was also a Frenchwoman, and an artist of works he'd admired for some time. He bowed.

"You honour me, Madame Vignée. However, I await one of your pupils."

"I am aware," replied the artist as she eyed the empty chair. Henry wavered foolishly a moment before understanding her hint. Once they were both seated, she nodded imperiously at a waiter before delivering her order in rapid-fire French. The young man blinked, nodded, and departed under the force of her formidable glare. The presence of such a talent, it seemed, had struck him dumb as well.

"We will have their *poulet à la Marengo*," she told Henry. "You will enjoy it, Major, as a refined gentleman." She smiled as her eyes slipped over Henry's epaulettes. Apparently, Madame Vignée was well-informed regarding English officers. "Traversant sends his apologies," she continued. "He is unavoidably detained."

"Perhaps you will assist me regardless," Henry suggested.

Madame Vignèe's gaze slid irresistibly over his left shoulder. "I will do my best, Major. You have a commission?"

"Perhaps," replied Henry. "I had the great pleasure of viewing your *Kassandra* at Christie's a fortnight ago. It is *magnifique*."

Madam Vignèe did not blush. She merely nodded. "*Merci*, Major. It is one of my favourite pieces. Tell me, is it sold?"

Henry shook his head. "I intend to be there for the bidding." He smiled at the delight on Madame Vignèe's face. Henry listened as the artist discussed her work and how she came to choose such a subject. Sure enough, the opening he'd awaited presented itself.

"The girl's hair was so vibrant," Madame Vignèe enthused. "I saw her as my Kassandra in a moment."

"The model must be very beautiful." He did his best to sound disinterested, despite every muscle in his body tightening with tension.

"Extraordinary, is she not?" Madame Vignèe appeared to sharpen her glance, and Henry had the uncomfortable sensation he was under examination. He'd not felt such intimate scrutiny since he'd been an ensign. He shifted in his seat, wondering if he dared pour out the wine. The covers were brought over, and there was silence for a few moments as they tasted their meal.

"However did you find her?"

"Her lodging house did not like her to return. She came to me some weeks after Easter," the artist replied. "Looking for work."

This timing tallied with the cessation of correspondence on Louisa's side—and the birth of her child if the babe lived. Louisa had likely been in health then. Henry allowed himself the tiniest of exhalations. "Does she feature in many other works?"

"Sadly, I do not know," Madame Vignèe replied. "My pupil surpasses me in influence." She attempted a self-deprecating laugh, which did not suit her.

"I beg your pardon, Madame?"

"I understand the girl—I do not recall her name—lives under the protection of Monsieur Traversant."

"Do you know if she remains in Paris?" It was an effort worthy of Keane to moderate his tone to one of tolerable indifference.

Madame Vignèe shrugged. "Traversant has the keeping of her. I know nothing more about her at all, Major. It is not in her interests to associate elsewhere."

"And Monsieur Traversant?"

Madame Vignèe repeated her shrug. "I attend you on his behalf. For the fees," she replied, carefully folding her napkin. Henry thought she glanced keenly in his direction, but when he faced her, she was waving to another diner. The stage had lost a talented actress when Madame Vignée decided to pursue painting. Still, if she was Traversant's agent, and this Frenchman had the keeping of his Louisa, Henry might contrive to get his godfather's family to safety after all.

"The commission I offer comes from the Congress," he ventured. "A historical occasion requires a serious genre artist, I'm sure you'll agree."

"*Oui*, Major. How is *le congrès* proceeding?"

Henry offered up his most diplomatic smile. "I cannot discuss specifics, Madame. I *can* offer your pupil and his entourage safe passage to Vienna." He held his breath. *Can she tell I'm bluffing?*

Madame Vignèe swallowed the last of her chicken. "This is most generous, Major." She sipped some wine. "I'd no idea *le congrès* was so well-resourced."

Henry bit back an involuntary smile. "You are quite the diplomatist yourself, Madame," he replied, without flinching. He felt, again, her minute examination of his every feature, as though the future of France could be mapped in his countenance. Her eyes, he noticed, were the most shockingly piercing blue. He doubted he'd faced a bayonet with sharper precision. Her head moved—a tiny, barely perceptible jerk of her head. A nod; agreement? *Can reclaiming Louisa truly be this easy?* Hardly daring to hope, he tasted his wine.

"Do we have an accord?"

"*Non*," his companion declared. "Monsieur Traversant cannot be persuaded to leave Paris at present. His admission to *l'Académie* is imminent."

Clearly this mattered a great deal to Traversant and to his agent. Henry supposed great sums and sales might be involved.

"Might your pupil be persuaded once his admission piece is complete?" He poured them both more wine.

"Mm," Madame Vignèe affected to demur. "*Il est possible*, Major. Once he submits, there is truly no requirement to remain in the city. Art flourishes as well in Vienna." Her smile appeared strained.

Henry repressed a shiver of awareness as the hairs on the back of his neck stood on end. Focusing closely on Madame Vignèe's expression, he noticed she looked—was it frightened? Traversant's agent was not nearly as disinterested as she claimed.

"What is the piece?" he asked.

"*Je vous demande pardon*, Major?"

Henry stifled a sigh, smiling winningly instead. "I have attended several lectures at which you spoke, Madame. I am well aware your English is excellent." He allowed his smile to betray the faintest weariness. "I've had a long journey overland, and should you care for dessert, you ought to know that my patience is not endless."

The faintest pink stained Madame's cheeks. *Progress at last.*

"I believe it is an historical major. Monsieur Traversant still seeks the right form."

"Form?"

"He seeks a male model. *L'empereur* may be raising his army again." She nodded at the look on his face. "*Oui*, Major, these rumours are all over Paris. Young men are not lining up to feature in exhibits for *art*."

"Then allow me to offer myself." Was that his voice? *How urgently do I want to find Louisa?* He remembered his unanswered letter and set his jaw.

"As what, Major?"

"As Traversant's model." *Urgently enough, apparently.*

Henry watched the woman opposite him blink slowly for a moment.

"Will I do?" he asked when no other response was forthcoming. His dining companion rapped on the table, full command of her faculties seemingly restored.

"Stand, please."

Henry looked around. "Here?"

"*Oui*." Madame Vignèe met his gaze and stared straight back, her blue eyes narrowing. "Art does not *wait*, Major."

With a resigned sigh, he rose.

"Turn," she commanded.

Henry's eyebrows rose. "Madame—"

"Silence!" Another command. This one accompanied by a raised palm as her eyes travelled over his profile, top to toe and then sideways.

He blinked at her evident appreciation—and his own disinterest.

"You are a handsome man, Major."

"Thank you." Henry cleared his throat. "May I sit?"

"*Pas encore*," she waved her hand. "Other side."

A vision of the General flew through his mind as he considered Madame Vignèe. He tried not to grin at the comparison.

"I feel as if I'm on parade," he muttered, turning as more heat crept past his collar.

Madame Vignèe's only response was a sort of low humming emanating from the back of her throat.

One of the waiters approached. "Major? Madame? May I be of assistance?"

Henry sat down immediately, but Madame Vignèe coolly delivered their dessert order. "Do you wish for coffee, Major?"

"*Oui*, Madame." Henry felt more like a schoolboy than ever. Watching the stares of other diners slowly withdraw, he unclenched his jaw and turned his gaze straight ahead—on another Vignèe, as it happened, this one a still life of cakes and roses.

"Well, Madame? Do we have *un accord*, as you would say?" He resisted the urge to hold his breath.

"*Oui*, major." She nodded as their desserts arrived. Touching her chocolates lightly on all sides with a fork, as though tuning an instrument, she concluded negotiations. "I shall make all the arrangements. You may report to the studio at *le Louvre* tomorrow at noon."

"I will meet with Traversant?"

"You will meet with Traversant." Those sharp blue eyes suddenly locked their gaze on his. "I am most pleased, major. I believe you will do very well for—my pupil."

Something in the way those eyes pierced him anew did not quite make sense to Henry, but he was too distracted to examine this further. His heart began a slow, triumphant beat. *One step closer to Louisa.*

Chapter 7

It wasn't difficult to trail Madame Vignée through the freezing Paris streets. Henry waited in the shadow of a darkened doorway and watched her leave, glad of the new moon's barely there light. Her scarlet cloak was quickly lost among many similar garments, but her feathered turban allowed him to keep her in sight easily enough. It was still early, and the streets were crowded. With the wars over and merchants beginning to offer more, the city was preparing for a truly merry Christmas. Henry found himself hurrying to keep his quarry in sight—he'd never have expected a woman of Vignée's vintage to be so spry. She slipped into an emporium, forcing him to take refuge in a nearby lane. He stood in the cold, hugging himself through his caped officer's coat and breathing over his gloved hands until she exited. A rapid walk onwards brought them to the imposing façade of *le Louvre*, where Henry again sought shelter in an obliging laneway. Shivering in the December night, Henry stared up at the windows, wondering whether Louisa was housed somewhere within.

"*Chocolat, monsieur?*" An old lacemaker huddled over a brazier as she worked her craft. Henry nodded and held out his coin, staring into the crowded darkness of the tiny thoroughfare.

"Do you require two cups?" She nodded towards the nearby crowd without smiling. "There are young women over there."

There were indeed several young women, smiling and winking among the foxed young men lounging by the entrance to a small establishment. Henry attended to the women closely. Some of them—most, in truth—were clearly whores and he was glad not to notice Louisa among them. He watched the older woman behind her fabricant, a cheroot burning slowly down between her lips. *I wonder...*

"Have you seen Monsieur Traversant today?"

"*Oui*, monsieur." She tugged on her skein. "In there." The woman jerked her head towards the doorway of the apartments.

"Does he engage many models?"

"Not there," replied the woman, with a vehement jerk of her head in the same direction. "This is not the residence of Monsieur Traversant."

Henry stared back, a puzzled frown on his face. "I beg your pardon, Madame? He has engaged me for *le Louvre*."

The woman shrugged. "Monsieur Traversant does not live at *le Louvre*."

"But you have seen—" he insisted, a horrible sensation taking up residence in his chest.

"He visits *le Louvre* only for the apartments of *la mademoiselle*. They say he is her *patron*." She all but spat the word.

"Patron?"

"However," his voluble companion replied, "I do not believe it."

"Why do you not believe it? Many fine artists live off the largesse of wealthy patrons."

The old woman shook her head. "Not so much since *la terreur*, monsieur, and few artists can support a student. An artist's 'patron' does not enter her rooms at dusk and remain until dawn. He does not leave in the same clothing in which he entered." She pursed her lips, and it was clear the lacemaker thought none too well of Traversant, or his mademoiselle.

Good God, this was worse than he'd feared. Henry's first thought was how he might break such news to his godfather. His second was to call Traversant out this very evening.

"The mademoiselle's name?" he asked urgently, hearing steel in his voice. "Do you know this?"

"Certainly, I do not know her." The woman turned back to her weaving. "Lace, monsieur?"

Henry adjusted his stance, felt about in his jacket, and located a coin. "*Oui*, Madame. Lace, if you please."

"*Merci*." She pocketed his coin then unravelled a lace piece from her apron.

"*La mademoiselle*?" Henry reached for another coin.

The woman shook her head. "I've not heard her called any name at all, sir. I saw her once at a private salon. I did not stay. I do not like the historicals. No clothes." She raised her grey brows meaningfully, offering up a significant sniff.

Henry held his breath. It had to be Louisa. His Louisa, another man's mistress. He couldn't imagine her consenting to such an arrangement, unless she thought herself alone, abandoned. *Why would she believe anything else?* Acidic rage churning deep within threatened to upend his guts.

He clenched his fist behind his back. "What does she look like?"

The woman chewed her lips. "I couldn't get near her for the fuss made of the painting she was a-posing beside. *La Madone et l'enfant* is scandalous, monsieur. She was all but ejected when the unveiling came off. Madame Vignèe was expelled."

"*Expelled?* What for?"

"Blasphemy, monsieur. The painting depicts *la mademoiselle*'s very own bastard in place of the Christ child. Vignèe's not attended her studio since."

Without another word, Henry handed the woman a coin and returned to his lodgings. He found his friend readying himself for bed.

"You are late to bed, Major. Does this mean you have sighted your quarry?"

Henry shrugged himself free of his caped coat, shaking his head before shooting the baron a black look.

"But then, where is it you've been? It is not to be supposed you were adding to your Traversant collection?"

"There's no chance of that," Henry replied and ran through the relatable parts of his evening. "It is possible my friend is lost," he concluded heavily.

"To be certain one way or the other, you will pose for this Frenchman's work?" His friend cocked his head to stare, as though Henry were a work of art. "Your determination to aid your lady painter is inspiring."

"Do you think so, baron? I am starting to consider my agreement as the actions of a madman. Or a fool."

"Or a man who loves," said the baron, very quietly. "It was your poet who said every man is a fool for love."

In no mood for Shakespeare, Henry merely grunted in response.

The baron gave up his considered stare, reaching for the bell. "I see you are still too angry for sleep. I shall have something sent up. Cognac, perhaps, and a deck of cards?"

"I am not angry, baron. I am *concerned.*"

"In Paris, cognac is the cure for both," his friend replied promptly. "Cards, of course, cures only my pocketbook, but I am willing to allow this."

"I appreciate the offer, baron. I shall likely make a poor companion."

"Of course. This is why we *must* sip cognac with our card play." He smiled.

Henry turned away to hide his irritation. *Very well, I'm angry* and *jealous.* Must he be transparent as well?

"Do not give up hope, Major. Christmas is a season for miracles."

Henry managed a smile as the knock came. "A miracle will be very welcome, as will cognac and cards. There is nothing more to be done this night." Until he saw Louisa, there was no telling how great a miracle might be required.

***

Louisa stared at her tutor, aghast. "I am fully aware I am under obligations to you, Madame, but this is—I am not sure I know the word," she went on. "This—this will undo all our work, Madame. It is *téméraire.* Reckless." She sank onto the divan, burying her face in her hands.

"You have found the word," her friend replied calmly, attempting to drag her side of the divan into position. Louisa rose to assist.

"There is no need for concern," Madame added, working on Louisa's bindings now. "You will wear your cavalier hat, with your false moustaches and your goatee. You will sit at your easel over there." She gestured vaguely at the far side of the studio. "The English officer will pose for you here." She pointed to the floor at her feet, where the afternoon sun usually lit the space with soft, golden light. "Enough space between you for any artist to create her illusion, *n'est-il pas si?*

Louisa shrugged. There was no arguing with Madame. The woman had talked her way into exhibiting in the Paris Salon at the age of fifteen. She was certainly proof against any objections Louisa may make. Angling the divan into position, Louisa resumed shaking her head as Madame gathered items into an enormous basket.

"I negotiated a handsome commission for you, *n'est-il pas si*? Besides, this Englishman, he is the model your work requires. Not merely handsome, but beautiful. The dark curls, and his soft blue eyes so full of love," she explained, kissing her fingers. "The moment Cupid grows into a young man beside his Psyche—it is a moment of passion becoming something more, *n'est-il pas si*? It is *le devenir de l'amour*."

"*Le devenir de l'amour*?" Louisa echoed, as though repeating an ancient chant.

"*Précisément*. This is the moment you will paint with this model."

"*The Becoming of Love*," Louisa said the title again in English, speaking slowly and with dawning wonder. A vision formed in her mind's eye. "I suppose this *could* work. *L'Académie*—"

"Will adore it, you know they will. *The Becoming of Love. This* is your title. I have arranged it all, Louisa." Madame shot a glance at the clock, threw up her hands, and buckled her basket. "This is not about any obligation, Louisa. This is about you, *mon coeur*. This man is the Cupid your art *needs*."

Louisa eyed the clock as well. *The English officer arrives in under an hour.* Her stomach twisted inside her. It was uncannily like her breeding illness, except she most certainly was not pregnant. No, this was sheer, unadulterated panic.

"Madame, I am afraid," she whispered.

"Of course you are." Her teacher's perfect understanding only confused Louisa further. "I told you, *mon amie*," Madame sighed, "art is about *truth*."

"So you are sending an English officer with orders to disrobe before me to find truth?" Louisa might have laughed if it would not dislodge her false moustaches—and if she were not so wary of seeing a man without his clothes again, even *as* a man.

"*De rien*." Madame gathered her basket in one arm and Henri in the other, planting a noisy kiss soundly on his forehead before making for the door. "You are welcome."

"You did not tell me his name," Louisa called out as Madame settled Henri more comfortably into her shoulder.

"Oh, he is a major. His name is the same as your son." Her tutor was already out the door. "Did I not say?" Gazing back at her with a last, penetrating stare from those frighteningly intelligent eyes,

Madame pulled the studio door closed, leaving Louisa—or rather, Traversant—alone.

"*Henry?*" Louisa exclaimed, sinking back onto the divan with her posture so slumped she may as well have been a French artist in his cups. An English major named Henry. *It can't be...*

Now that the wars were over, Henry ought to be at Clayford. Still, how many majors could there be with such a penchant for fine art that it drew him to the first *Salon de Noël* in years? Louisa leaned her head back and took a deep breath. Would she be able to deceive her oldest acquaintance? They'd not met for an age. *Perhaps, if I keep my distance...* She looked around the studio, nodding to herself. *I shall use what I have.* What did she have? Her art, her art was all. The *mise en scène* would be in the light. Her placement was behind the easel, in shadow. Her colours were mixed, and some were now thickening. She scurried about, reorganising the room into a place that offered the most cover for herself, still thinking. There was very little need for a model to see the artist up close. Quite the reverse, though...*do I wish to see him?*

Of course she did—her favourite friend, and the man she held in highest regard, come to sit for her. For as long as she could remember, Henry's kindness distinguished him among the other gentlemen of her acquaintance. He always seemed to be assisting her achievements in some respect. Her father's permission for an artistic master had been given at Henry's urging: the General would not likely have yielded to his daughter's entreaties alone. For the rest of her life, no matter how it went on, Louisa could not think of Henry with anything other than gratitude—and some small measure of regret.

Guilt flashed through her as she glanced at the pile of unopened correspondence. Further communiqués to Henry were well overdue. Her light, laughing-style letters regarding her "continental holiday" were little more than lies. Louisa had not the heart to distress her friend with current truths. Besides, she'd not heard from him for several weeks, and she thought she knew why.

Henry must know. He'd have found out the moment he returned to Clayford. The General ordered her cast off, and Henry was, after all, under his godfather's command. Her old friend was a cautious man. He could not approve her now, nor admit her society. Ruined, reckless, and foolish, could she ever hope to know previous acquaintance again? *What must he think of me?* Taking up her Traversant costume with a sigh, she blinked back tears. Her regrets regarding Henry were not small at all.

Slipping into a pair of modified breeches, Louisa bound her breasts in several layers until they presented as flat as possible beneath the man's linen she'd sewn. Over all of this, she donned a jacket thickened with padding to portray shoulders and a male physique. Leaning down, she pulled on her riding boots. Finally, she eyed herself critically in the enormous mirror.

Can anyone tell I'm myself? Not for the first time did Louisa reflect on the irony that living life on her terms required several layers of disguise. To be herself meant no one else must know Louisa existed. The sting of tears in the depths of her eyes was best shaken away.

"I'm being ridiculous," she said aloud. "And I am certainly not about to cry. The moment I answer his knock with swollen eyes, I am undone." She took a breath and then another. *Steady.*

Her final act was to don the overlarge cavalier hat that hid her false moustaches and goatee from line of sight. It was not convenient to wear such a hat while creating but needs must. If she could paint while eight months pregnant, she could do it wearing a hat, while doing her best to avoid thinking of her old friend. *Friend?*

Closing her eyes, she was transported, lost in a memory she'd tried vainly to forget. In truth, the moment was terrifying to recall, because it was a fateful day. The day she almost lost the boy she'd loved for all of her life.

The boy's body tumbles into rushing water...a sickening splash and her screams. No help to be had. Within moments, her torn gown and petticoat lies beside tossed slippers and stockings. She parts icy waters wearing only her chemise. Swift, strong strokes fight the current until she reaches the river's centre. Inhaling deeply, she holds it, ducking for as long as she can. Nothing. Surfacing, she breathes out, breathes in, diving down again. A foot, a hand, a curl of red ribboning the water—his head. He's hit his head. Swimming with the current is his only chance. He's too heavy otherwise. Grabbing his arm, she strokes for the bank, nearly dragged under with the weight of him.

Louisa opened her eyes, remembering that Henry left for Cambridge the next day, sporting nothing worse than a bruised forehead. She didn't see him again for over a year. Not until the following Easter. Sketching by the Cam, where they—*but some memories are best forgotten*. Her father's godson was a grown man now, a soldier. The memory likely loomed far larger for her than for Henry. *And yet, he still writes.* Her conscience pricked.

Blinking hard, she laid out poppy seed oil and horsehair brushes.

Chapter 8

"You are sitting for your Frenchman today?" Von Humboldt's commiserations were as unnecessary as his apologies for winning at cards the previous evening.

"It is my own doing, baron." Henry had slept soundly and faced his day with renewed purpose. He was certain he'd learn more about Louisa at Traversant's studio. "I have time to visit *La Salon* this morning if you are not engaged?"

"I should be delighted," his friend replied. "There are no few samples of Traversant's art to study if you wish more research."

"This is a good idea," Henry agreed as a knock came at their door. "I do hope that's breakfast."

"It is indeed, Major. I took the liberty of ordering for us both."

"I am much obliged." Henry took up his linen, glancing hopefully at the water jug. "Is there hot water?"

Von Humboldt smiled. "There was, Major. The water is brought up promptly at eight, but I can ring again."

Henry shrugged. "It's as well England has allies such as yourself, baron. Imagine if the French wished to do battle before our dinner hour."

His friend laughed and ordered more hot water from the maid.

"Do hurry," Henry called after her, checking his fob. There was much he needed to achieve before he met with Traversant.

***

It was a quarter to twelve when Henry entered the *Grande Gallerie* of *le Louvre*. He studied the other young men awaiting their artists, doubting anyone would take him for a model on sight. His posture was too correct for one thing. It had been many years since he'd sat for a portrait.

The last time was when he'd been awarded his commission. That formal and very correct work now graced the library wall at Clayford, along with his father's and no few of his godfather's. Uncle George had had several portraits of himself hung at Clayford—one for each promotion. One could never accuse the General of immodesty. Henry found posing for his single sitting in full military dress more than enough. Sitting for Louisa had been an entirely different experience. He smiled reminiscently.

Another moment and Henry rapped sharply on the relevant apartment's door, careful to place his fists in his pocket. It was only by reminding himself that this was likely Louisa's home that he managed to subdue his fury at all. He hoped he could sit still enough to be painted, while resisting the urge to go several rounds of bare-knuckle with Traversant. He knocked again.

The door opened, and he stared at the auburn-haired gentleman before him. He was a mere youth. Traversant must be several years younger than himself. He was pretty too, in a way that seemed to favour so many of the younger, slighter fellows. A fashion Henry could not appreciate, as he was not slight, slim, or lithe. Henry was a soldier and of a larger frame than most. *This* was the man who seduced Louisa in Cologne? *One punch will fell this milksop.*

"Good afternoon," he began with a bow, reminding himself not to land a blow.

Traversant cleared his throat, bowing in his turn, though his large hat remained. He stood aside, waving Henry in. For some reason, the artist seemed to gaze at his model's boots rather than his face. Ushering him behind a screen, he indicated Henry ought to disrobe. There was not much in the separated space: a narrow bed placed closely beside a single chair, and a small tallboy. He spotted a washbasin and jug, a lamp, one tiny armoire, and a cradle. *This might be Louisa's home.* The place appeared clean, at least. Henry stared at the cradle for a long time. *Louisa deserves better.*

He'd not been asked to pose yet. Slight noises from the other side of the screen indicated his host was readying his palette over by the easel. The man was so silent, Henry thought he might not know English.

"I beg your pardon, monsieur, do you speak English?"

"*Oui*," came a gravelly voice that sounded far too soft. "Yes. I have—er—something wrong with my throat." He banged on his slight chest, coughing like an invalid. "Please, complete your dress," Traversant requested into the tensely quiet room.

Henry looked down at himself and around. He was as naked as possible—that is to say, entirely, but—*what the devil?* A leather harness lay beside him. The device supported two man-sized wings, created with actual feathers. It was artistic, elegant, and beautiful. It was also the least masculine object Henry had ever seen.

"What is our subject?" he inquired politely.

The Frenchman cleared his throat again. "Cupid and Psyche."

It was Henry's turn to cough. He thought he drew the line at feathers. *Apparently not.*

He attempted to buckle himself in several times before calling out. "I—I believe I require your assistance, Traversant." *If the Frenchman laughs, I* will *strike his pretty face.*

He heard a sigh as the artist approached from across the room, seemingly studying his own boots this time. Traversant held the wings in place, cinching the buckles until Henry winced. The costume was loosened immediately.

"I beg your pardon." Henry heard the man mutter—and thought he detected a strange accent. The hands smoothing his wings into place were paint-stained but elegant. Henry took a degree of comfort in their slight tremor.

"How do you want me?" he managed to ask, annoyed at his nervousness.

"You have sat before, Major?" Traversant uttered his first complete sentence.

Henry withheld his applause. "I have, sir. As a student."

"*Bon.*" The artist yanked him into a space lit by an obliging sunbeam. At least it was warmer. Henry glanced down. The studio was rather cold, and it showed. He counted back how many years since he'd posed like this. *Cambridge,* but he hadn't removed all his clothes for Louisa. Though he'd very much wanted to. *Hmmm*…perhaps now was not the best time to revive those sensations.

"All right then." Reaching a hesitant hand across, the artist pushed Henry's shoulder into position. His palm was light and cool, with the faintest hint of lemon-scented soap. Henry started: *Dear God, Traversant is the most delicious-smelling Frenchman I've ever—*

Bloody hell, he'd never.

There oughtn't to be anything erotic about being tugged into place by a slightly built French youth, yet the hands that positioned him were so soft. So careful, as though the artist was afraid of offending him. *Or arousing him?*

Henry swallowed hard, astonished. He'd had no idea an artist's hands would feel soft. Did they not roughen their skin with turpentine and varnish? How on earth could a man's hands feel like this? How could a man's touch inspire such a response from him—if *inspire* was the word? He focused his eyes directly ahead, noticing an unfinished canvas. The sketch was difficult to make out, but he thought he recognised the gabled rooftop: *Clayford*. He shook his head. *It can't be.*

Traversant trailed an appreciative fingertip along his chest, pulling him gently into place. Henry's fingers clenched, gripping the cloth draped artistically across his hips. The silks suddenly seemed inadequate to their purpose. They were not enough, and in the same moment, far too much. The chill of the studio receded as Henry's body responded with heat, and— He froze, which was gratifying, as artist's models are not supposed to move—or harden.

"There," Traversant murmured. "Now you're precisely where I want you."

"Where's that?" Henry asked, swallowing hard.

"Where Cupid first seduced his Psyche, of course."

Henry smiled to cover his discomfort. "I always thought the point of that myth was that it was the other way around."

"I beg your pardon?" The artist spoke without looking at him.

Henry thought he detected something novel in his tone. The man sounded unsteady. *What is he hiding?* Henry would bet his major's pay it had something to do with Louisa. Returning to the conversation at hand, he watched his companion as closely as he could, given his head was turned a certain way. He did not wish to ruin what promised to be a spectacular work of art.

"Did—did she not rather seduce him?"

"I think not," replied his host. "He was the first of the two to love, I believe."

"She was the first to break faith," Henry countered, surprising himself with the depth of feeling in his words. "If Psyche had only waited, she might have been spared so much suffering."

"Then she would not have become as divine as her mate," came the reply. "Cupid, too, becomes full-grown only in the presence of a love beyond the physical. He is transformed through her love for him."

"Despite her betrayal?"

He thought Traversant flinched. "The betrayal is as much his as it is hers, Major. He wanted her, he took her, and he ran from her, leaving her alone. Hardly honourable."

"Hardly," Henry agreed, his tone fiercer than he intended.

"She was asked not to know him," replied the quiet voice behind the easel. "Not one lover in a thousand could do it and still love."

"No mortal lover, certainly," Henry said. "Her lover was divine."

"She is not aware of this in the myth," Traversant pointed out. "What woman may assume awareness in safety?"

Henry was silent for a long moment. "One who trusts her lover completely," he replied softly, unsure if he was speaking to the Frenchman now, or simply himself.

"Do you speak from personal experience, Major?"

The *astute* Frenchman. It was Henry's turn to flinch. He cleared his throat in response, catching a glimpse of guilt in the artist's eyes—and fear. That shivering sensation crept up his neck again, startlingly familiar. Something had happened here, and by God, he meant to find out what. *This cub will know Louisa still has friends in this world. Friends?* Henry forced this thought away. Louisa was his friend, his family, the woman he loved—and he'd not give up now.

"Have you visited England, Traversant?"

"*Non, monsieur,*" came the whispered reply.

"Why are you whispering?" It was then he realised he was whispering, too. What the hell *was* this? Henry cleared his throat, and it seemed too loud. "Traversant?"

The Frenchman's head popped out from behind his easel before ducking away, dark eyes flashing beneath the brim of his ridiculous hat. "Silence, please," came the low-voiced command.

Henry acquiesced, listening to the rhythmic scratching of chalk on canvas. Sitting still for long periods had seemed less troublesome when he'd been a student. Louisa had not required silence for her work, and she had noticeable talent. He studied a completed still life, presumably placed for drying. Louisa's art had been at least as good.

It took him a moment to realise Traversant was humming. *Humming*, while his model stood there in a state of semi-arousal, and—Henry glanced down again. *Very well, not so semi.* He'd never been more grateful for drapery in his life, but now he was even more bloody confused. He turned his thoughts to battle. To England, politics, and the General, expelling a relieved sigh when this did the trick. After what seemed an age, the sunbeam completed its retreat, and restraining his shivering became impossible. Three chimes from across the Seine indicated they'd been at work for three hours, and Traversant called a halt.

"You may stand down, Major." The artist placed his materials beside him and stood to stretch. "This is all for today. You will dress if you please."

The Frenchman seemed to be waiting for something. After a moment, his host stepped forward and unbuckled the wings, his fingers running lightly over Henry's torso, as though by accident. Henry repressed a shiver of response to the scent of lemons again. Should the man not smell of something less, well, *lovely*? He turned his attention to finishing his dress as rapidly as possible, while the artist hurried back behind his easel as though it were a shield. *As well you might*, Henry scowled. Except that the man's manners lacked refinement, he'd learned little regarding Louisa.

"Shall I return tomorrow?"

"*Oui*," Traversant replied. "If you can arrive a little earlier, there is urgency around this work now."

"Oh?"

"This piece is for admission to *l'Académie*. I understand you are not likely to remain in Paris long. Is this so?"

"I am here at least until Christmas, monsieur."

"*Bon*," Traversant replied. "It is enough."

He said nothing more after that, indicating that Henry ought to let himself out.

***

No more than a half-hour later, the door opened to admit Madame and a slumbering Henri.

"I suggest to leave him in my basket, *mon amie,*" Madame whispered. "He is sleeping like the lamb of God himself." She smiled down at the infant and back up at Louisa.

Louisa smiled back and nodded. No need to disturb such a well-earned rest—for any of them.

"Madame, may I consult you?" she said, nodding toward her easel.

"Of course," her friend replied. "We must hurry. I am not supposed to stay at *le Louvre.* What is your concern?"

"The painting is proceeding well. The model, he is—"

Madame kissed her fingers. "*Superbe,* is he not?"

Louisa's cheeks warmed under those clever blue eyes.

"Ah, you desire him. My Louisa will finally *love.*" Madame embraced her but Louisa did not respond.

"It's not that, Madame."

"You do not find him *beau*?" Madame looked shocked. "I cannot believe this."

Louisa shook her head, holding one hand aloft. "Madame, Cupid is an old acquaintance of mine. He is *Henry.*" She raised her voice, glancing over at her son.

"*L'Anglais* who writes you such lengthy *belles lettres*?"

"The same."

Madame clasped her hands together. "But this is excellent," she exclaimed. "It is like a miracle. A Christmas gift. *Love*, at last. Love for my Louisa."

"*Madame*," Louisa interrupted her raptures. "This is Henry. H-he knows me too well. It is most awkward."

Madame did not seem to grasp the significance. "What is this concern? You are a beautiful woman. He is a handsome man. You desire each other. Always, you make the objections, Louisa. One would think you did not wish to take a lover."

"Perhaps I do not."

Madame shrugged her shoulders and rolled her eyes in tandem. "I will not permit foolishness in my studio. I tell you, Louisa, this is a place for *truth*. For love."

"Which is it, Madame, truth, or love?" The urgency in her voice frightened her.

Madame shook her head, clearly irritated. "*Mon Dieu*, my greatest student is indeed a fool. Tell me something, do you trust this man?"

"Oh yes," Louisa replied without hesitation. "There is no man I trust more than Henry."

"Do you know, *mon amie*, how many people spend all their lives searching for a lover like the one you describe? One who knows them *intimement*, and in whom they may safely place their faith?" Madame Vignée's eyes took on a wistful cast. "Before *la terreur*, I was wedded to such a love. I do not expect to meet such as he again," she concluded softly.

Taking Louisa's hands, her teacher gazed fondly into her face. "You have trusted too many who were not worthy of your faith, Louisa. Do not now turn from one who is. You *deserve* his love, my dear. That is, if you want him."

"If I want him," Louisa repeated. *Do I?* "But what if he realises *I* am Traversant?" She clutched at her palette. "Henry is no fool."

Madame shrugged. "You say you trust him. I have met this man and I, too, trust him. He will not betray you."

"You sound so certain."

Madame twitched a shoulder. "He will not incur the wrath of Madame Vignée." She smiled, and it was entirely without amusement. "I am like you, Louisa."

"Like me, Madame?"

"*Oui*. I fight fiercely for the ones I love."

And you have lost more than enough. Louisa pulled her friend into an embrace then.

"Dear Madame," she whispered.

The moment her friend left, Louisa sank to the floor, pulling her disguise away from her face. *Henry, why must it be Henry?*

"Of *all* people," she lamented aloud, staring furiously at the ceiling. *Of all men.* She studied the work she'd completed that afternoon. Madame was not wrong: Henry was the right model for Cupid as a young man. The god of love, stretching into his full masculine form in the presence of his truest love and soul companion. The uniting of physical desire and something more ethereal, a divine aspect, was a quality she'd always associated with Henry…*my Henry*. Louisa shivered with a sort of delicious alarm.

She'd thought of him this way for so many years, had even dared to hope once that he might return such a love.

"That is all over now," she told her Cupid-Henry. "I will complete this work, turn down the Viennese commission, and that is that."

Whatever Major Musgrave wanted from her—from *Traversant*—Louisa must ensure he left her life here intact. There must be no more chat about divine mating or thwarted lovers. No further distractions at all. An image of Henry's torso appeared before her. Louisa shook her head. She was an artist and a professional. She must not allow the beauty of a man whose kiss seared her memory to distract her, nor the planes of his handsome face, or the way his dark hair curled at his collar. She must certainly avoid noticing his impressive arousal. Louisa blushed, blinking as though this erased such an image. *No chance.*

"I will complete my work in as few sittings as possible," she promised her painted figures. Then all would be as it was before her old friend had arrived in her studio, removed his clothes, and sat for her alter ego—with wings. Louisa snorted as she recalled the expression on Henry's face when he realised he was posing for Cupid.

"That was almost worth it all." She laughed aloud as she worked the spaces between the god and his lover, hoping to complete her carbon black lines before Henri required more milk.

Chapter 9

The taste of her, honey and pears, softly bold lips opening beneath his...the power of her kiss, the quickening beat of his heart as his mouth meets hers. Breathlessness, the freshness of her lemon-scented skin, gently shifting breasts against his chest as he holds her. The silken feel of her cheek beneath his palm. That look in her eyes. Melting brown, lit with amber fire. Her expression brimming with certainty, grace, and her trust in his kiss—Traversant's face blurring in and out of focus, as though he had something to say about this kiss. As though it was as much his as Henry's...

Henry awoke, scowling at this infuriating finish to what had been a truly sensational dream. He glanced across at the other bed, noting that the baron had already left. A polite note on Henry's valise informed him that their Hôtel Westminster "served breakfast only until ten." Folding his hands behind his head, Henry noticed a little stiffness from sitting too long in a single attitude the previous day. He wiggled his hips beneath the blankets, but his arousal remained. *After dreaming of Traversant?* This fascination for a Frenchman was the last thing he needed. *Fascination? Bloody hell.*

Throwing off his covers, he began his morning preparation. The water was cold, but he didn't bother ringing for hot. The mantel clock showed he'd best stir himself if he did not wish to disappoint his Frenchman. *His?* Henry swore loudly and rang for coffee.

***

More humming accompanied their second sitting, and Henry grew used to the aroma of turpentine again. Traversant kept him at it until after one o'clock, when he called a halt.

"You may take some refreshment, Major." His host nodded toward an assortment of boards on which breads and fruits lay artistically arranged. *No meat?* Henry presumed this was an artistic conceit and took up an apple.

His artist stood. "I shall fetch your wine."

"That will be most welcome," Henry replied, rising to a stretch as he twisted his head from side to side. He saw Traversant's gaze shift, following the movement of his shoulders and back. Henry did his best not to react. He did wonder, though, what a man of Traversant's habits wanted with Louisa as his mistress. This Frenchman was quite the puzzle.

Traversant bowed and exited, turning at the door to issue his gravel-toned directive. "You are not to look at my easel."

Henry reached for his breeches. The moment Traversant left, he was on his feet, moving around the room to learn what he could from the works in various stages of completion. Behind one sheet, he found a baroque mirror covering an entire wall. Henry could only imagine what purpose that might serve. Despite the artist's prohibition, he stepped behind the easel and saw that Cupid's mate was already sketched and partially painted in. Tumbling red curls, long, lithe limbs—and a familiar butterfly birthmark.

Careful not to touch the works in progress, he found racked canvases in another corner. Henry turned them cautiously around, examining them closely. Nudes, each and every one. Nudes of a woman with auburn curls—and the same lissom shape he remembered—turning away from the viewer like the painting at the Dorotheum. Traversant's model faced *into* the canvas. As though she didn't want anyone to see her—*or he doesn't*.

Facing the last three paintings outward, Henry let his gaze wander from one to the other. A series featuring the same model, with each image intimately unique. The first showed the woman turning three-fourths away, her breast towards the viewer, offering a plump, tight nipple, and her face turned inwards. The second foregrounded her curved thighs, one knee raised as the woman reached for herself, her breasts falling forward. The third—Henry almost blushed. Her body arcing in ecstasy as she touched herself, legs splayed, her head thrown back, a hint of wide lips, her face obscured by those fiery curls. She was undeniably arresting—and arousing—and still, the viewer could not know her.

Henry ignored the tightening of his body, studying this final image until each brush stroke imprinted on his memory—including those depicting a mark on the womanly thigh. He leaned in as close as he dared. There could be no doubt. A butterfly-shaped birthmark, the exact shade of his favourite claret.

"Louisa." He said her name out loud, turning as the door opened behind him.

Traversant balanced a cut-glass decanter, the wine colour matching the birthmark precisely. Rage exploded in Henry's gut. Crossing the room in two quick strides, he gripped the lousy French youth by the shoulders.

"What have you done with her?" he demanded, jolting the decanter until glass shards exploded over his bare feet, spilled wine seeping across the floor like blood.

"Goddamnit!"

"Henry." A terrified expression met his harsh gaze—deep brown, lit to the depths with amber, and that mouth...*her* mouth. Louisa's voice and her mouth—Henry held the fellow tighter, his brain struggling to find sense.

"What is this?" He staggered backward, grimacing with pain.

Louisa looked down. "Oh gracious, oh no. Henry, don't move." She stepped away, and with surprising strength, managed to drag the divan into place. "You'd best sit down."

"*You'd* best explain yourself," Henry warned, nevertheless sinking to a sitting position. "It is you, isn't it, Louisa?"

An uncertain laugh sounded as her hand came up. With a tug, her moustaches and goatee were gone. Her face was Louisa's once again, though garbed as a man. Henry tried not to grin—and failed. That winsome face of hers, so close to his own, and she was here with him, and she appeared well. It wouldn't do to speak his heart out loud. *Not yet.*

"It's truly lovely to see you," he blurted—and his anxieties dissipated like sun-warmed mist. "I take it you're *not* Traversant's mistress, *la mademoiselle*?" He was only half-amused when Louisa shook her head.

"I-I," she blushed and stammered, keeping her eyes on the divan. "How is—" She gestured vaguely towards the smashed glass.

Henry shook his head. "I've suffered worse, and it doesn't matter." He reached for her hand, trying not to mind when she recoiled. "This does," he continued. "*You* do. To me, you do, and I want you to know that."

***

She watched his hand reach out to push an errant curl away from her face, saw he meant to tuck it under her hat, which he did, but not before he'd twined it around his finger and stroked its length, sending tiny shivers of heat from her scalp to her toes. Louisa shifted her head away, pulling off her oversize hat. Next, she peeled away the skull cap, shaking out her curls.

"Louisa?" He threaded his fingers through hers, warming her skin by several degrees. *Warming? It's as though I burn with fever.*

"I do not know what I can say in this moment." Her voice sounded faint, as though she were speaking at a great distance from her body. She opened and closed her lips, issuing several gurgling sounds that might have been words.

"Why don't I begin?" Henry said gently. "How is your child?"

Louisa's eyes widened in shock. Stunned into deeper silence, she simply stared at him. This beautiful-bodied man, here in her studio— with those ridiculous wings strapped to his back. She bit her lip to stop herself smiling.

"Is something amusing you?" Henry asked. "Or are you forgetting I know every expression that moves your face?"

"Clearly," she replied, staring now at her paint-stained hands. "I expected interrogations, accusations. Possibly some form of recrimination." She fixed her gaze on his face. "Apart from Madame, you are the only one who has asked about my son." Something like rage flashed in Henry's eyes and she found this reassuring.

"Your child is a boy?" He grimaced, his gaze falling to the glass shards littering the wood floor. "I beg your pardon, Louisa." He swallowed. "I would wish you'd not had to bear so much."

She spoke into the overloaded silence. "Henry?"

"Yes, Louisa?"

"Why are you here?"

"The General sent me to bring you to safety," he replied. "Bonaparte may yet return, and—"

"All of Paris knows these rumours," she interrupted. "If that is all—"

"But you asked why *I* am here." Henry stood, making his way gingerly over broken glass pieces to the little table beside the refreshments. Taking up the large pile of correspondence, he flipped methodically through her post.

"My personal correspondence?" Louisa stood, her voice rising. "What do you think you're doing, Henry?"

"There are several here from the General." Henry's reproach showed in his face. "Unopened, I see."

Louisa stared back at him, determined not to address this sally. "I have nothing to say he could want to hear." The harshness in her tone surprised even her.

"His anger is long since done away, Louisa."

"Mine is not." She held his gaze. "The price of his returned favour is not one to which I willingly submit."

"And my favour, Louisa?" Henry continued turning over her letters, pausing when he seemed to find the missive he sought. "This is *my* personal correspondence."

"What is it you mean?"

"My last letter to you," he answered, holding it aloft. "To which I have not yet received a response. *This* is why I am here, Louisa." He held out the carefully folded foolscap.

Louisa's astonishment overtook her irritation, her heartbeat picking up noticeably. She stared at the letter…*Henry's letter.* She was strangely reluctant to take it. Holding it warily, she fingered the regimental shield impressed into the seal.

"Th-thank you. It must have become muddled with the General's letters when I changed residences." Her gaze met his, her tone soft. "You must know I did not intend to offend you."

Henry expelled a breath. "I returned from the wars to find you 'on the continent.' That's all I was told, until—"

"Until you saw the General," Louisa broke in, her voice cracking. "What did he tell you?"

"That you were in a certain condition," he replied quietly. "So you went away."

"Was *sent*," Louisa corrected, her tone souring. "Banished."

"Yes," Henry agreed. He looked down at his hands as though he could read palms. When he next spoke, he sounded raw. "In all the time we corresponded, my dear, you did not mention any of this." He turned his head, looking into her eyes. "Why?"

Louisa's cheeks burned far more at the pain in Henry's voice than with the memory of her shame. He was almost her best friend.

Friend? She shrugged inwardly. She did not know if there was a word for it, but they'd been so close. She shut her eyes for a moment and took a breath. When she opened them again, she could not meet his gaze.

"I—I could not put it into words." Louisa stared at her shoes or his bare feet. Or, possibly, the shattered glass shards littering the studio floor. *A metaphor.*

"Writing it down would have made it too—" She hesitated.

"Real?" Henry finished for her.

She nodded, reaching for his hand. "Your letters were my lifeline, Henry." She squeezed his fingers, looking earnestly into his face. "Please know that. There were days your words were all that kept me—" she choked to a stop, shivering like a frightened thing.

He reached for her other hand then, pulling her into his arms, rubbing slow circles over her back.

"Louisa," he sighed, shifting until she nestled easily against his shoulder, and she was comfortable. The solid warmth of his chest beneath her cheek was a harbour in the storm her life had become. Glancing up at him, she relaxed in a way she'd not done for far too long.

"Thank you, Henry," she sighed, grateful for his warm, firm presence. For his rare ability to listen, without judgment, to her fears and choices. "Truly, there is no one else like you." She sat up, touching her palm to his cheek, offering a small, soft smile. "How I've missed your presence, these many months away."

Her smile deepened when he smiled back, tipping his face in minute increments towards hers. Time slowed down as she held herself still, determined to receive him, to trust him, to learn how he wished to love her.

His lips touched hers gently, reverently, and the sweetness she'd held in her heart for so long was still there. *Here, he's here, with me.* Part of her, part of *them*, rejoiced as he lifted his fingers and traced the sensitive line of her jaw.

"Your skin is so soft," he whispered as he drew back, teasing the corner of her lips with his thumb. "Beautiful Louisa."

He leaned in again, and the boy from Clayford, the sweet young man from Cambridge, was kissing her. The soldier from the wars, her Cupid, was kissing her. Without demand, without judgment, with nothing but his mouth on hers and his heart thudding against her own. Louisa tugged him closer until his lips settled over hers, his tongue flickering in and out over her own, firing each nerve into tingling molten shivers, spreading outward like ripples on a pond. Her lips parted as he deepened his possession of her mouth.

A tiny sound escaped her as he pulled her close, pressing firmly against her. Dimly, she wondered why she was not afraid—and then she remembered. *This is* Henry. Her Henry, his fingertips skating the length of her neck, edging her collarbone with tender, gentle caresses as he traced intricate patterns over her skin.

Louisa stroked his chest with her palm, feeling his breath quicken, the leap of desire shifting back and forth between them like a sparking tinder, and oh she'd dreamed of this, of him, and that it seemed to be coming true at last. She nestled closer for a moment more before pulling her lips from his, breathless and panting as though she'd run a race. The heat pinking her cheeks must surely be from midsummer, despite the chill creeping through her studio this close to Christmas.

"M-my son will be here soon, Henry. We'd best continue your sitting tomorrow." Without another word, she began unfastening his wings.

Henry smiled, never taking his eyes from hers. "As you wish, Louisa." He kissed her again once, dressed, and stood to bow. "Tomorrow morning?"

"If you'd be so kind," Louisa replied, bowing in her turn.

Henry grinned. "A fine bow, Monsieur Traversant."

Louisa shot him a dark look that she could not maintain. In a moment, she was shaking her head and snorting with laughter. Reaching up, she settled his cravat as she used to do at Clayford.

"Thank you," said her Henry. "May we speak more tomorrow?"

Louisa nodded, attending him to the door. She looked up at him. "Henry?"

His eyes stared down at her, warm and honourable.

"It is truly lovely to see you as well."

"Perhaps you might read my letter, Louisa. When you feel ready." He bowed again and left her alone.

***

Once she'd disposed of the broken glass and mopped up the lamented wine, Louisa stood before her easel, turning Henry's letter over and over in her hands. *When you feel ready*, he'd said. Well, that moment was not now, Louisa reminded herself briskly. Placing the paper carefully behind the frame of her last completed piece, she returned to studying her day's work. Madame would be back with Henri in a short while. Louisa must make the best use of the time she had. She leaned in, her finest brush loaded with whitened yellow ochre flecked with gold. Holding her breath, she traced the love god's quiver, limning his feathered arrows. Sitting back, she nodded to herself, making a mental note to visit with her colourist before tomorrow's sitting. She needed more gold to create the effect she wanted for her lovers. The flecks were not cheap, but Louisa was determined to find a way. This piece deserved it.

After two sittings, she had the design ready and the sensual languor she sought to capture for Psyche. There was nothing erotic about the work though, at least not yet. *Does there need to be?* Louisa tutted at herself: *Cupid is the god of physical love.* Her work ought to reflect this. She already knew what Madame would say: "What are you afraid of, Louisa?" *I am afraid of this feeling...this feeling I am not sure is love.*

Madame and Henri made their appearance shortly afterward, and Louisa settled her hungrily groping child at her breast. Madame sat opposite her for a moment, head tilted to one side as she studied the pair of them.

"I do not care for the objections of *l'Académie.* My *Madone et l'enfant is* religious, and she is beautiful." Her teacher smiled, then straightened suddenly.

"Louisa, Traversant's lips were not vermilion this morning."

Louisa blushed and Madame laughed with triumph. "He saw you," she decided. "He saw *you* today, not Traversant. Do I have this correct?"

"*Oui*, Madame." Louisa's cheeks were like a furnace. "Please do not—"

"There were kisses," her teacher spoke with a faraway look in her eye, as though her information came from tea leaves or divine inspiration. "And now you will take him for a lover."

"Madame, I cannot."

Madame raised her palm. "Do not speak to me of your English objections. The Englishman desires you. I was aware of it when we dined. You desire him. I'll hear no more about it until he has taken you."

Louisa shook her head and turned the subject as best she could. "Madame, I wish to speak with you about the work. Something is missing. It is movement and light and flow. It is not—it is not *love*."

Madame looked pityingly back at her. "Of course not, Louisa. You must be loved to paint love. You must *allow* love."

"One imagines I have done so," Louisa replied drily, switching Henri to her other breast.

Madame uttered a rude noise. "That is not love, Louisa, as any man with a heart can tell you. Your Henry will not be so gauche."

"He is not my Henry," she denied it, but could not help her next query. "Gauche?"

"The major's appreciation shows his heart." Madame ignored Louisa's shake of the head. "Henri's father, did he admire your work?"

Louisa almost laughed. "No," she replied in a low voice. "I do not believe he knew of my paintings. Mostly he admired himself."

"He did not know *you*. Your Henry, you say he is not like this?"

"Henry knows everything about me," Louisa said absently. *Or at least he used to. I've not written...* She flushed. Henry's pain became her own. She'd hurt him—unintentionally, and with the most clear-sighted reasoning, but she couldn't bear it.

Madame's next words were almost inaudible. "I do not pry, Louisa. I do not seek to know which man hurt you so deeply, but I know this. Your Henry has a true heart. He understands you. This is a rare gift in a lover."

"Madame, I cannot take a lover," Louisa repeated. "Henri—"

"Deserves a mama who is happy and well-loved. You deserve this too, Louisa. As does your art." Madame Vignée indicated the easel with an imperious lift of her head. "Your admission piece will not be all it can be unless it depicts love. You are painting Cupid and Psyche. Divine love, and a lesson in trust. Your work must show this, or it will not pass."

Louisa sighed. "Thank you, Madame, but I have no intention of becoming mistress to an English officer. How can you know Henry desires this?"

Madame stared as though she thought Louisa was touched. "Tell me, Louisa, how were his *wings*?"

Louisa thinned her lips to stop her laughter, and it was only Henri's nodding little head that subdued her hilarity.

***

Later that night when her son was abed, Louisa studied her work again. Staring at her miniature model of Canova's famous sculpture, she shifted her gaze between statue and canvas repeatedly. Henry's physique precisely matched that of the divine god's. Louisa's tongue slowly stroked over her lips, remembering his mouth on hers, the warmth of his touch, the heat of his gaze when he looked at her.

Major Henry Musgrave, with wings. She added dabs of lead white to the feathered appendages, considering Madame's words. Louisa knew several gentlemen with an appreciation for art, but few who might encourage her pursuit of it in so passionate a manner. None she could persuade to costume himself in such an outrageous fashion. Only her dearest friend would champion her so. Only Henry would don feathers to aid her. *Only Henry.*

Chapter 10

Henry considered it a great pity that, while Louisa dispensed with her hat and hair cap the next day, she still dressed as her alter ego, lest someone call for Traversant. Disappointed though he was, keeping his desires in check did seem easier than if she wore a bodice. He spent the morning keeping himself stationary, wondering what devices Louisa employed to ensure she appeared so slight in her upper body. Her painted nudes clearly indicated otherwise.

"What else did Papa tell you?" Louisa asked him as she set out their luncheon at the noon break.

Henry watched her eyes, which showed shame, fear, fury, and sadness. He also saw strength and defiance. When she looked back at him with softness, he could have shouted for joy, but that wasn't what he wished to talk about right now.

"He said you'd been seduced," Henry spoke carefully.

Louisa's tiny, bitter laugh seemed to hurt her lips. "Seduced? Well, I suppose it sounds better than 'let herself be taken.'"

"He forced you?" Henry's jaw clenched. *I'll kill him and any dukes who get in my way.*

Her strangled laugh came again.

"I have no wish to pain you further." He gentled his voice with an effort. "You do not need to tell me unless you wish it."

"I am only afraid of what you must think of me," she said, her voice very low.

He took her hand. "You are still Louisa." He kissed her knuckles. Turning her hand in his, he kissed her palm, feeling a slow breath move through her.

"I was encouraged to permit his acquaintance at first. He is—considered very great. He persuaded me to believe in him. In his care for me," Louisa whispered with a shudder. "I was—mistaken." She stopped speaking. Her shuddering did not stop.

"Come here, dearest." His palms slipped around her waist as he pressed her to his chest, stroking her hair. She didn't release him, and a moment later, a tentative palm touched his jaw, tilting his head down until her mouth met his. Then his lips slid over hers, tonguing her mouth open as his mouth played gentle games with hers. He sucked on her lower lip, drawing her closer until his palms curved over her buttocks and his mouth found her earlobe. Her breath came hot and gasping against his ear, and he might have come then and there, merely from the proximity of her skin to his.

"Henry, I did not mean—I cannot," she whispered. "I need more time. It is not because I do not want to. Please, know this at once."

He nodded, breathing like a bellows before her. He drew back, gulping air and panting hard. It took fully ten minutes for his breathing to return to a semblance of sanity. He was silent for a long moment.

"I do not wish to seem indelicate," he said when she'd recovered enough to resume eating. "The General claims you will not name the man."

Louisa's cheeks reddened. "As I told Papa, to do so places our family at great risk. A risk that now, necessarily, includes my son. This I will not do."

"So you will carry this weight alone?" Henry stared at her in horrified sympathy.

Louisa looked away. "To think that I should see you again after so many years, only to shame myself in your eyes." She spoke almost to herself, covering her mouth with her hand.

"The shame is not yours, Louisa. It is his. It is—" Henry took her hand in his again. "It is too much."

"If you cannot countenance an acquaintance such as I, you may leave me to my fate." She dropped his hand and stood then, upright and proud. Henry easily witnessed a vision of Kassandra in her stance. He fought an absurd desire to kneel.

"I mean it is too much for *you*," he amended gently. "Why do you insist on carrying all this pain alone?"

"I am stronger than you may believe." The flash of defiance in her eyes reminded him again of the Trojan seeress.

"I do not doubt you," Henry replied with feeling. "He is not worth your protection."

"You misunderstand me. It is not for his sake that I keep quiet," she insisted.

"Nevertheless, your silence protects him. Give him up, Louisa."

"So the General may have satisfaction?" Louisa shook her head.

"So that all who care for you may find satisfaction in protecting you properly." He spoke tenderly, though his expression might have been fearsome, judging by the alarm in Louisa's eyes.

"No, Henry," Louisa replied in a low voice. "It will not serve, you know. This way, the risk is entirely my own. Name him, and I leave my child open to his claim on the boy." She glanced toward the cradle, shaking her head again. "If the scandal were known, I'd have heard of it. I receive correspondence as regular as yours from another acquaintance. You know the delight with which some ladies inform on others, regarding ill consequence."

An expression of distaste crossed Henry's face and he tried again to moderate his tone. "I know your—situation—was no accident. As I mentioned in my last letter but one, the Duke of Carston still screens the man responsible."

"To keep his heirs from the front lines," Louisa confirmed. "I am aware."

"Carston presumes upon the General's wish to avert a scandal, to demand favours in Whitehall."

Louisa's cheeks flushed with anger. "It is my child Papa cannot countenance. He would have hushed up my being seduced, but a baby cannot be hidden."

"What a nonsense. There are dozens of ways to—"

"I will not do it." She stood there, fists clenched at her sides, high colour in her cheeks, fierce as a goddess herself. "This is why I cannot return to Clayford. I'll not give up my son."

"Who was born four months ago," Henry deduced.

"Nearer five, in truth. How did you—"

"Four months ago, you stopped replying to my letters," Henry said quietly. "You left the residence the General provided for you—"

"I left Cologne five months ago with Madame. My lodgings were only paid up until my confinement."

Henry blanched. "I never knew."

Louisa looked him full in the face. "I am aware Papa was greatly angered when I refused to foster my child. I do not regret it, though there were moments I feared how we might live."

"This is when you began to paint?"

"I have always painted. After Henri was born, I agreed to sit for Madame. She pays her models well."

Henry's gaze slid over her appreciatively. "This is how I came to find you. *Kassandra learns her fate* exhibited in Vienna."

"A visually arresting piece," Louisa recalled.

"A visually arousing model," Henry replied, with a grin that melted in the uncertainty on Louisa's face.

***

She attempted to glare admonishment at him and could not. She smiled—and devil take him, Henry smiled right back. A warmth she had not known in a year flooded her skin. She shook her head, still smiling. *Dear Henry.*

"I daresay the General did not intend to mislead me about your lodgings in Cologne," he added. "I left him in Vienna greatly distressed. He sent me on purpose to find you out and bring you home. My resolution, however, was already formed."

"Did he mention my son?"

Henry shook his head.

"I'll not return to England without my child." She may well be repeating this refrain until Henri came of age. *So be it.*

"Have you read my letter?" Henry persisted.

Why did his focus on an outdated letter make her nervous? *Why, indeed?*

"Do you seek to change my mind by post?"

"I seek your safety, Louisa, and your son's."

His calm unnerved her too. "Do you speak true?" Louisa asked aloud, wondering when the words "fallen woman" might pass his lips and his proposition make itself known. She swallowed, all the words she longed to speak uncontained, spilling from her eyes.

"Louisa." Henry took a step towards her.

Her head shot up, eyes glittering. "Do you mean to take me as your mistress?"

He blinked. "What an idea! You know I could never—"

Louisa's gaze fell to her feet, face burning. *What gentleman would take her, a disgraced daughter of society?*

"—disrespect you so," Henry finished.

Disrespect me*?*

"Then what is it you *do* mean, Henry?" she asked him baldly. "Let us have no more careful diplomacy. Why did you kiss me?"

"When I returned from the army, it was to you I wished to return, Louisa."

"Do you speak true?" she asked again, heart slamming against her rib cage so heavily she felt weak, shaken, and a thousand other sensations in a moment. Was this *hope*—and with it, fear? Louisa looked into his face and found fear lived there too.

"Henry?" she ventured, her voice a mere breath.

"Will you read your letter?" Henry suggested, blue eyes burning with dangerously familiar intensity. "Please," he added in a whisper, staring at her mouth again.

Is this what the poets mean by learning to trust? Watching this man who'd grown out of the boy she'd always known, always trusted, Louisa understood Psyche more intimately than Canova ever could have. *If he kisses me again, I am lost.* She blinked, remembering that she'd already lost her standing in society—and only Henry had sought her out since. *Only Henry.*

She crossed the studio and retrieved the envelope. Taking up her palette knife, Louisa broke the seal and read:

July 1814
Calais

Dearest Louisa,

My return from France is unavoidably delayed. I cannot detest the packets enough. I am sorrier than I can say to have missed Easter with you at Clayford. I seek to make amends, you see, by writing three letters to your single response. It seems this way, at least. I understand you are touring Switzerland and Prussia. I wish you much pleasure in your journey and consider whether this be the reason for the pause in your letters.

It is too many weeks since I have had the pleasure of hearing from you. While it is not in my nature to barrage you with inky declarations, I do not like the shadow of reserve hovering over our correspondence of late.

I do not mean to scold you, either. Your letters from Clayford mean a great deal to me, as indeed do you. I hope my meaning is not obscured nor my intent disabled. I dream you closer when reading your gentle words. To have our intimacy disrupted by the continental post is bearable; to suspect it curtailed by your choice is less so—far less.

I wish to know whether your heart is as changed as your geography, or does it remain, like my own, firm and true? My less assured heart is too often uncertain, except in one respect—the way it hammers when I'm in your company, or spy your hand on any paper I've kept, that I might read it over again, or when I think of you, as I do a hundred times each day. Or when I dream of you, but this I cannot write without your acceptance of the below. This, then, is the subject of my third letter in as many weeks.

Know this, dear, sweet Louisa: I seek both your hand and your heart.

I await your response with trepidation, hope, and the kind of beauty that can only be my love for you.

This certainty within my breast has ever been thus, and it is yours. I am yours. That is, if you wish to be mine.

Do you, Louisa?

Your (if only you'll have me),

Henry.

Oh! She could not speak. Louisa tried smiling but it was an anxious, twisted expression.

"Henry?" She seemed to be holding her breath.

"Yes, Louisa?"

"You wrote that letter before you knew—" she stammered. "Before you knew that I am—"

"That you're what?" Henry responded impatiently.

"Ruined," Louisa whispered, as though pronouncing a prophetic curse on her own fate. "Your playfellow from Clayford is grown up. Into a f-fallen woman."

"Tell Traversant that if he refers to you in that way again, he shall meet me." That ferocity flared in his face again. There was no jest in his words. Only gentleness and a kind of quiet power.

Louisa looked into Henry's face, seeing his kindness and love—and his unyielding determination. She released her breath in a rush. "How do you always know the right thing to say?"

"Only to you," Henry responded, and this time he did kneel, reaching up to take her hand. "Among others I seem a bumbling sort of fool. Only with you do I feel like myself. Only with you am I the man I have always aspired to become, dear, sweet Louisa. Fix me in this betterment and make one man good forever."

"You wish this still?" *Even now?* She could not help her astonishment, though her fingers twined through his. "I am hardly the sort of woman you're supposed to wed," she said, still tugging at his hand. "Disgraced. Depraved."

"Do not say such things about the woman I love." Henry stood, stepping forward to take her other hand. Pressing his lips to her forehead, he stood back, stroking her fingers with his own.

"You're *you*, Louisa," he corrected quietly. "Tell me this is unchanged, and my heart remains as resolute as it ever was."

Louisa simply stared at him, a slow joy rising within her. This man—this *good* man, one of the best of his kind she'd ever met with—wanted to marry her.

"Henry, are you certain?" The warmth of his larger hands seemed to seep through her skin.

"If I'd come home sooner," he asked gently, "would you have consented to a betrothal?"

"Oh, Henry." The look in her eyes conveyed all the reassurance he needed.

"Then I am the greatest fool who ever lived," he declared, as the bells of Saint-Pierre chimed the hour.

"That's our luncheon over," Henry said smilingly. "What's next for your work?"

Louisa thought for a moment. "I don't think I've discussed the work with you, as I usually do with my models."

"I understand artists like to take their models to bed. By all means, treat me accordingly."

Louisa chose to ignore this charm, though her gaze slid studiously over his torso. Not for nothing did Madame call him *superbe*. At twenty-five and army-fit, he was a truly beautiful man. Louisa cleared her throat, nodding towards her clay model. "I am painting my version of Canova's sculpture. Do you know it?"

"I know it. *Psyche Revived by Cupid's Kiss* is one of the looted works now resident at *le Louvre*. I saw the prime in Rome years ago. A fitting subject for your admission piece." He glanced at the divan, then returned a look that had Louisa blushing in an instant. "Where do you want me?"

"On the divan," Louisa replied without thinking, then gasped in horror when Henry chuckled. "Tell me, Major Musgrave." She coughed to cover her embarrassment. "When did you become so bold?"

Henry grinned, admiring the clay statuette of the famous sculpture. "Canova's Cupid descends from the sky, reaching down towards his mate. Psyche lies supine beneath him, reaching upwards as she wakes to her lover hovering above, clasping her breast. Their lips barely touch, positioned almost upside down from each other because, of course, your love god is in flight."

"This is correct," Louisa replied. "But you did not answer my question."

"As you have not answered mine," Henry returned levelly. "I am a patient man."

Louisa raised a brow as she looked at him. "Then you are, in truth, much altered, dear Henry."

Henry raked a hand through his hair. "Very well then, I am not patient at all. Awaiting your response is already the most painful exercise I've endured to date, and I've faced Bonaparte in battle."

"Henry…" Louisa began, but he raised his palm in surrender.

"You've borne a great deal, Louisa. I will not add to your burdens. If you need time, you shall have it, my dear." He smiled at her with a look that was hungry rather than complacent. "Meanwhile, let us get on with your work. I am as keen as you are to see this piece completed."

Louisa exhaled with relief. "Thank you, Henry."

"And to have you beneath me on your divan," he added, so quietly it was almost a whisper. Her body's response was to bloom with heat, as though she stood too close to the fireplace—which was not lit, due to the scarcity of fuel. She shook her head at her foolishness, mumbling an apology as she hurried forward to make amends with a precious taper.

"You're not disrobing?" Henry's curiosity was quite undone by the desire in his eyes.

"It isn't necessary," Louisa replied, her face flaming. "I work on Psyche's image at night, via lamplight. She is nearly complete, modelled on my reflection." She indicated the enormous mirror.

Henry raised a disbelieving brow. "Then how will you adjust for relative scale?"

Louisa knew he was right. She closed her eyes and opened them again. Modelling Psyche with Henry above her sounded like temptation. What might occur when she lay beneath him? *Love.* A love she could trust? She remembered Madame's advice. *You must be loved to paint love.*

"Very well," she almost mouthed the words, stepping behind the silk screen. She removed her boots and stockings first, then her breeches. Her modified linen took but a moment, but she had difficulty when it came to the rest of her costume.

"Damn." She swore softly and jumped when Henry's shadow appeared on the other side of the screen. He was quite tall enough to see over the entire structure but had turned his back. *Only Henry.*

"May I be of assistance?" He managed to sound like a modiste.

"I've had to strap down for Traversant," she explained.

Henry made a sort of choking sound in response.

"Are you laughing at me?"

"Not at all," came his reply. "It's such a shame to disguise your—,"

"My *seins*?" This time she could have sworn Henry's choke was to keep *his* propriety in check.

"Er, I intended to say 'curves', but yes."

"I'm about to lie practically naked beneath you," Louisa said drily, though her voice trailed off with her breath. "I think we're both adult enough to use the correct terms."

Henry laughed outright. "Do you think the French term less risqué?"

"I've heard more bawdy expressions among Traversant's fellow artists." Louisa moved out from behind the screen, presenting him with her back. Henry began unknotting the tight cloth.

"Girodet's speech thoroughly shocked me the first time I sat down with him as Traversant."

"I can imagine," Henry murmured. "Unlike your fellow artists, I am in no doubt you are a woman."

His breath warmed her neck, creating a deeper heat low down in her body. Telling herself to shake off such a sensation was useless. She didn't want it gone. She wanted it hotter. A delicious thrill rose within her, a sensation she'd never thought to trust again. *Such dangerous enchantment.*

Slowly she removed the rest of her disguise, aware of Henry watching each gesture. At last, her shoulders were bare, and she stood naked from the waist down. All that remained were her bindings.

"As I said," he repeated softly. "What a shame."

Aware of the charged silence, she did her best to fill it.

"Traversant was Madame's idea."

"I've no doubt."

"She did it for me," Louisa went on. "Only four women per year are admitted to *l'Académie*, and their quota is met. The wars made it far less likely for an unknown like myself to have a chance of it, so Madame suggested I apply as her male student. I receive better prices for my work as a man as well, and I have my child to provide for."

"This explains Traversant's reputation as something of a recluse," Henry added.

"It is not to be supposed that people will remain fooled for very long. I appear as Traversant only when necessary. I am aware it is not strictly honest, but—"

"Compared with the politics of Europe, the subterfuge of two artistic ladies barely merits a raised brow from me, I assure you." Henry commented.

"Ah," he exclaimed in triumph as her bindings loosened. He spun her around repeatedly, twirling the suffocating wraps as though the two of them were engaged in a new dance unknown to any other couple. Louisa laughed aloud at the dizziness. A moment later, he spun her free, and she laughed again, her chest rising and falling with her last encumbrance as he gazed at her.

"You're not meeting my eyes," she pointed out, watching his reflection in the mirror.

"Can you blame me?" He twined her wraps around his hands until she stood before him, lit from behind by the afternoon sun and perfectly outlined in a final layer of thinnest muslin. With a visible effort, he drew his gaze from her form to her face. "Beautiful Louisa," he said aloud, staring directly into her eyes.

"You are not moving," Louisa observed, her voice a tremble of hopes and fears.

"I promised you time," he answered, still holding her gaze, blue eyes flaring with heat, and something else. Something warm, and wonderful, and directed entirely at her…oh, dare she trust again? Dare she trust *this* man? *Only Henry.*

Her heart breathed a prayer, and she hoped her hands stopped shaking by the time she picked up her brushes. Clearing her throat, she attempted to regain control.

"Regarding your letter—"

"Proposal," Henry interrupted, his voice thickening. "It is a proposal of marriage, Louisa. I think we're both adult enough to use the correct term," he chided gently.

"Very well," she acceded. "Regarding your proposal then, I'll not leave Paris before my admission piece is submitted. The work is too far advanced."

"No more should you," Henry replied firmly. "I insist you complete it. *Properly*," he emphasised, moving across to the divan.

"Whatever do you mean?" Louisa seemed to have lost her ability to speak above a hush, though her model's intent was obvious from the way he balanced himself on his forearms.

"Cupid is positioned thus, and you did not know the relative balance and—ahem—size of your male model until I agreed to pose," he began, leaning adroitly above a non-existent Psyche. He exhaled for a beat, then turned his head to gaze at her. "Well, Louisa? Are we creating art, or not?"

She moved slowly towards him, as though drawn by some unseen force. Laying herself on the divan, she gazed upwards into Henry's eyes—and beheld a power there, a heated determination that drove all the breath from her body.

"I believe Psyche appears nude." Henry's voice seemed deeper. It was definitely warmer. A careful tug at her last, loosened wrappings, and they fell entirely away. Henry kicked them aside, the slight movement of his thigh muscle startling—and enticing.

This is Henry. *My Henry…if there's a man you can trust not to desert you, this is he. Only Henry.* Her pulse throbbed at her throat as though a fever burned through her, and her fears receded, strangely distant, as though she had, indeed, been charmed by love's arrow—because she knew what this was. What this must be…*love*.

Chapter 11

Henry stared down at her, his words sharper, warmer, and somehow closer. "It's not the first time you've taken my likeness."

"You're thinking of Cambridge," she guessed, watching his eyes darken.

"Are you reading my thoughts now?"

"Not exactly," she replied, a wicked inspiration seizing her as she slid a palm over the curve of his buttock, shaping the tight muscles of his thigh. "I have some thoughts of my own."

Henry growled low in his throat. "Louisa," he groaned.

She stroked his thigh, delighting in the catch of his breath. "Did you love me, then?"

"You saved my life, Louisa. I've loved you always."

"Then why did you enlist?" She couldn't help asking.

"I don't know," he mused. "You were not yet out and far too young. We were both so young, and I had no prospects. No family. I had nothing."

"Is that all?" Her palm stopped moving, and it seemed he breathed again, closing his eyes momentarily. "Madame says this studio is a place for truth." *Honesty, please, Henry. Honesty for me, and for yourself.*

When he looked at her again, his darker blue irises widening in a heated stare, he seemed to hear her thoughts. He stayed silent for a long while. When he did speak, his voice shook, and his words seemed to come from a deeply hidden place. "I'd already lost one family, Louisa. I was barely a child when my parents died. I don't remember it very well, but I do remember being afraid. Almost all the time, until Uncle George made me his ward." He looked at her properly then, the expression in his eyes softer than she'd ever seen it. "I was afraid," he finished. "I wanted—I think I wanted to be enough for you."

"Henry," she whispered, threading her fingers through his. "You were always enough. You *are*."

Talking made no sense anymore. With a heartfelt sigh, Louisa raised her arms in the pose she'd studied for weeks upon weeks now, as her winged mate reached towards her, his lips hovering inches above her own. She pushed upwards, her lips meeting his, and Henry leaned down, tasting her mouth…this was the same. The same kiss she'd carried in her heart for almost a decade—only it wasn't. Something was different, and she knew now what it was. His kiss, his lips—he was no longer the boy she'd grown up with at Clayford. This was Henry, full-bodied man, with his knowing mouth, his muscular hardness, and a passion matching her own. A passion she'd been fortunate to find when she was fifteen and did not know what she'd awakened—but she knew it now.

He slid his hands down over her belly, drawing her hips upward, until her gasping breaths were all she heard, and his mouth pinned hers in a tangle of tasting, touching that had her aching for more. It was the same touch, the same caresses from her Henry, all hot, fierce desire from this man who wanted her, who wanted her to want him, and she did. She knew him, wanted him, wanted Henry. Her love. Her home. Her heart, and as he found the taste of her, she could not let him go again.

Gentle lips caressed her, sensual touches as he drew her closer, closer, until his weight made it difficult to breathe and she rested her hand on his chest—oh god, his chest, his skin, the warmth of his body shifting above hers.

She did not push against him. No, she did not want to push him away. She wanted him closer, wanted to touch every part of him, and kiss his firm lips until he held her again. She kept her palm on his chest, undecided, tempted to rub her other palm over his thigh. Instead, she leaned up, tasting his torso with her mouth, feeling him shudder and moan. His muscles shifted beneath her palms as a power she'd not known she possessed filled her with heat and light, and a need for this man she'd wanted for so long.

Touching her tongue to his rib cage, she traced each rib, sliding her hand over disarranged drapery. Her lover made another sound—something between a cry and a groan as she kissed her way up his chest, his neck, and found his head thrown back. He stroked her hair, kissing behind her ear and whispering words she'd never heard a man say before. Placing his lips beside her ear, he told her all the ways he wanted her, all the pleasure he sought to give her. She wrapped her arms around him, hugging him tightly, her lips pressed firmly against his skin. She'd never felt safer or more loved. He felt like Home. He felt like hers—because of course, he was. *This* was Henry, the boy she loved who'd become an even better man—*and he still wanted her*. She almost pinched herself to be sure she wasn't dreaming.

The hard, hot length of him pressed against her. For a moment, she tensed.

"Shall I stop?" he whispered, his lips buried in her neck as she writhed against him.

"Henry," she moaned. "Henry, don't stop, please." She opened her lips beneath his, pulling him into her, feeling him fill her, plunging himself deep inside her until she cried out, holding him closer, wrapping her legs around his hips. "Oh, Henry."

"Louisa." He stroked her cheek, taking her mouth in a searing kiss as he moved, the warmth of him filling her, growing hotter until Louisa could hardly stand it, crying her response into his shoulder when she shattered against his hardness. A moment later, Henry's release filled her, and she gasped in sheer delight.

He lay atop her, and for a moment, they breathed together. Then Henry moved aside, kneeling beside the divan. He traced her mouth with his finger, his gaze never leaving her face. She kissed his fingertips and stretched, more relaxed than she'd been in her whole life. She watched him watching her, his smile the warmest thing in the room. Louisa smiled back.

"Henry," she sighed happily. "Is it always like this?"

"Well, I am not certain Canova's statue is quite so dynamic."

Louisa laughed, the sound a husky echo. Henry lifted a stray curl from her cheek.

"I had no idea," she said then, speaking almost to herself. "It wasn't anything like this before."

"I should hope not," Henry's voice hardened. "Are you sure you won't tell me?"

"I do not wish to discuss it at all." Louisa's lips tightened a moment before she concluded. "There is no need to mention it again."

"No need?" Henry's hand made a fist of its own accord. "Louisa—"

"No, Henry." Louisa cut him off. "On no account will I name him. On no account are you to attempt to trace him. I'll not consider your proposal without your word to let this be."

Her voice echoed through the silent studio. Louisa thought she might hear the oil settling in her paints. Beside her, Henry breathed unevenly, as though mustering some sort of resolve. "Your requirement is not easy for a man to accept," he said at last.

Was that a catch in his voice?

"Nevertheless, I insist," she spoke gently. "I do not wish to offend you, but I will not risk my son."

"Your son. I do not even know his name."

It was Louisa's turn to gather herself. "His name is Henri."

"You named him Henri?"

His astonishment was worthy of a grin, but she felt too serious for that.

"Not George, after the General?"

"I named him for the best gentleman of my acquaintance," she said after a beat, noting the speed with which her pulse raced beneath her skin as she told him the truth of it. "I named him for you, dear Henry."

"For me?" Henry seemed dumbfounded, and at last Louisa had to smile.

"Is it so surprising?"

"Yes," he almost shouted. "I mean no. I mean, I do not think I am able to make meaning from this, but—you named him for *me*?"

How had she forgotten the joy of surprising Henry?

"So—so, not after his father?" He seemed intent on this point. Louisa could hardly blame him.

"No, Henry."

The silence returned, but with a different shade to it.

"Do you love him?" Henry asked after a long pause.

Louisa knew what this question cost the man beside her. She knew it in the tension of his muscles and the effort he made to keep the pain from his voice—and she knew her answer meant all. "He is nothing to me. This, I swear to you. I ask you to allow me freedom from my past and allow my son this protection."

Twisting her head to face him, she spoke with an intensity she prayed he believed. "I am honoured by your heart, Henry. I ask for your faith in mine likewise." She hoped he understood because she meant every word. No one knew better than her that words were only worth so much. "Please, Henry," she whispered against his mouth.

He shifted away. "*Did* you love him?"

Henry deserves the truth. Meeting his look straitly, she took a steadying breath. "I believed he loved me," she explained. "This is what seducers *do*, I understand. He led me to believe we were to be married. He pressed me to—to—" Her voice stumbled, and lying there, in the arms of a truly good man, she felt more sullied than she ever had before. Henry's beautiful eyes blurred in her vision, as though she'd marred her canvas like a Nazarene painter. His face dissolved almost completely as Louisa did her best not to show him her shame. Before she could say another word, she felt his finger against her mouth.

"Hush now," Henry whispered, though with an edge to his tone. "You need say no more, and there's an end of it. I give you my word. If you ever change your mind about seeking him out—"

"I won't." She stared up at him. "You do truly wish to marry me?"

Henry looked down into her face, puzzlement in every feature. "I should have thought that obvious. I love you, Louisa. We can be married here and return home afterward."

Resisting the urge to wrap her arms around herself, Louisa twisted her fingers together, pressing her knuckles until the bones cracked.

"Then the answer is no."

***

The air sizzled, Henry's skin shivering in the chilly aftermath of regret. The ensuing emptiness echoed with emotion.

"The answer is no," he repeated into the long, unquiet silence. "To the General, or to me?"

"To returning to Clayford." Louisa's voice lost all its warmth. "I'll not leave my son to be raised by strangers."

"And I'll not leave you unprotected in a city that's to be overrun." He rose slowly beside the divan.

"We are at an impasse, it seems." Louisa stood. Her flattened voice may have fooled others, but not Henry. *Like father, like daughter.* He studied her face, refusing to renounce hope.

"I remain in Paris until Christmas," he informed her in level tones. "Would you do me the honour of spending the season with me?"

Louisa blinked. "Surely you must know I do not intend to miss my child's first Christmas?"

"I assumed as much. Perhaps I might make his acquaintance at last?"

Louisa stared at him, a look of wonder filling her face. "Make his acquaintance? Henry, he is an infant."

"So much the better. I've always wished to spoil a child at Christmas." He spoke without ceremony. "All you need do is say yes."

"To Christmas?"

He hated the hesitation in her words. "To Christmas." *I promised to give you time.*

"Does the invitation include Madame?"

"It will be my honour to host you all." Henry bowed, feeling quite the cake as the weight of the winged harness dug into his flesh.

"Then I thank you," Louisa replied. "We shall be delighted. I have only agreed to Christmas, mind. Nothing else."

"Of course." Henry exhaled, unaware he'd been holding his breath. "After all, we've a work of art to complete, and I can't think of a better way to court an artist," he added with a grin he hoped conveyed at least as much charm as lust. When it came to Louisa, he doubted his subtlety.

"Do you mean to court me?"

Again, that uncertainty he could not wait to sweep away. "I believe I've made that clear." He flexed his shoulders. "Now that we've settled the holidays, may I remove these ridiculous wings?"

Louisa uttered a warm laugh, her focused gaze alternating between Henry's position and the perspective offered in the mirror opposite. "Not until I'm satisfied."

"That sounds like a challenge," Henry grumbled.

Louisa grinned, "Perhaps once I've completed your *shape*," she shot back, keeping her gaze on her model. She donned a silken wrap and took her place beside the easel.

He watched her at her paint table, adjusting lead white into red ochre, staring at the sunbeams as though they contained all the answers to her questions. She held her breath while mixing the vermilion for Psyche's lips, the tint a memory he felt in his soul.

"Can you tense your right shoulder slightly?"

"How's this?" Moving his shoulders into the light, he tightened the muscle as indicated.

"Quite all right now, thank you." She started to hum as Henry studied her, painting him naked. She worked quickly, layering each shade above the previous one so that it might dry in place by morning, building up the illusion of depth with variations in tone.

"Do you often work like this?"

"Yes, quite often. I pose before the large mirror you see, doing my best to create my female form. It requires something of contortion, but it saves francs to be my own model."

"You do this each night after I leave?"

"Yes."

"Naked?"

"Yes."

"You astound me."

"Ye– I mean, why?" She glanced at him, then returned to her work. "It is not to be supposed you are aware of how limited my time is with classes to attend at *le Louvre*, no few paid commissions on hand, and my babe to care for. Since Madame has been good enough to refer some smaller works, I do not pose as much as I used to."

"You have posed for other artists?" Henry asked faintly.

"I have only posed for Madame and for Monsieur Traversant. I could hardly maintain Traversant's disguise by sitting for anyone else." She laughed at him.

Henry tried not to smile at the sound he'd missed for so long— admitting to himself that this might be because, no matter her "society," Louisa was still Louisa. Some hearts remain forever unspoiled, and hers was one of them. For the first time since he'd learned her fate, he could be grateful to the fool who had not realised the value of the woman he'd dishonoured. *Not that I wouldn't call the blackguard out if I had the opportunity…* But he promised Louisa he'd let his anger die. She believed in him. *Then I must make this true.*

An image of his godfather flashed through his mind. Uncle George's sense of honour was less delicate than his daughter's. Henry stood somewhere between the two of them on this scale. He doubted subduing such primal inclination was in any man's nature, but he refused to be another man who let Louisa down.

"Flex to your left, please," she ordered.

Henry flexed his other shoulder, relaxing his right, doing his level best not to stare at her. Louisa, his lover and—possibly—his wife. This time, he would not leave without securing her promise to marry and leave the city. If she'd only accept him, he might finally possess the means to make Louisa safe forever.

"What are the plans for Christmas?" Louisa asked without lifting her gaze from her canvas.

"We can discuss that later." His deep drawl made her look up.

"I beg your pardon?"

"This isn't high tea, Louisa," Henry was only half-jesting. "This is art, and I wish to see you turn out a piece so stunning that those coxcombs at the Academy will fall at your feet and beg you to join their salon." His tone lightened. "If you require silence and focus, you need not entertain your model. Believe me, I have more than enough to consider." He almost smirked at her brazen exposure.

Louisa shrugged, blushed, and smiled. "Thank you, Henry," she murmured and there was no further speech for some time as she worked away, humming under her breath. When the church bells rang out for None, she downed tools and called to Henry to relax his pose. Louisa helped him dress, pressing tightly against him when he kissed her good night. The rightness of kissing her, of holding her to him, was as intoxicating as it was frightening.

Chapter 12

"I knew it," was Madame's triumphant declaration on reading Henry's letter. "Your Henry is charming and he writes well." She shot Louisa a shrewd look. "You've accepted him, of course?"

"We are engaged to spend Christmas with him, and his acquaintance, here in Paris," Louisa demurred.

"Why allow him to make love if you do not intend to accept him?" Madame Vignée asked bluntly. "I do not understand you English."

"This has nothing to do with my being English," Louisa spoke loudly. "This is about Henri. Henry spoke of marrying here and returning to Clayford. You know what that means for Henri." She could not soften her mode of expression any further. The idea of leaving her son...she would not do it. Not for any reason. *Nor for anyone.* Not even Henry.

"Has he said anything about Henri?" her teacher asked after a moment. "Has he refused to accept him?"

Louisa stared. "He did not precisely say that, no."

The older woman clapped her hands as though at the theatre. "Then, can we not allow him a little time, *mon amie*? This Christmas will be a delight. I am preparing *such* items for the little one."

Louisa smiled. "Madame, you are too good. Henri is so little. I pray you do not spoil him. He will not likely recall it."

"Forget his *Tante Vignée*? He'll do no such thing. I forbid this *petit*. Absolutely forbid it." She almost glared at the baby, who gurgled up at her with his gummy grin.

"There, you see?" Madame looked back at Louisa in triumph. "He will never forget his first Christmas in Paris. How can his *maman* be so foolish as to suggest such a scandalous thing?"

"*Le Salon de Noël* is reason enough to make this a holiday to remember, I suppose." Louisa smiled at Madame and Henri.

Glancing back at her painting, she narrowed her eyes and stepped back some distance.

"How goes the work?" her teacher asked.

"It is coming together," Louisa replied absently, tilting her head to one side. "Henry does indeed resemble his divine counterpart."

"He is what your art needs, my dear Louisa," Madame Vignée affirmed. "And what you need."

"I have agreed to Christmas," Louisa reminded her. "Nothing more."

Madame repeated her dismissive hand gestures. "We shall see what Henri makes of your major. You mentioned other acquaintances?"

"Baron von Humboldt accompanies Henry in Paris. A close friend, and a devoted collector of your works, I believe."

Madame Vignée smiled back at her like a beneficent Demeter. "An artists' Christmas, with two handsome art connoisseurs. *Is* there any greater felicity?"

"I did not inquire as to the baron's looks."

"Ah," said her friend. "He buys my art, so he is handsome enough. I need no viewing to determine this. Is he also the sort to pursue an unanswered betrothal letter all the way across the continent?"

Louisa laughed. "I understand he is already betrothed to an earl's sister."

"A pity," Madame replied with mock sadness. "Still, I will make the best of him. It is a talent of mine, making men better than they are, you know. You have this skill as well, Louisa."

Louisa stared, her mouth agape. "Henry said something very similar when we were—" She stopped, blushing so brilliantly that her painting tutor could not contain her glee.

"Now I find the secret of your rapidly accomplished brushwork today. Tell Madame, did you *paint* at all?" She laughed again at Louisa's stammers of protest. "He is good for you, this Henry, and astute as well," Madame said. "May I ask, Louisa, what it is you are so afraid of?"

Louisa squeezed her eyes tight shut and shook her head. "It's been a long day, Madame." She opened her eyes. "I must feed Henri and rest. My Cupid returns tomorrow." *My Cupid?* Louisa staved off a determined shudder. *This is* Henry.

"For his answer, I presume." Madame would not be deterred.

Louisa expelled a breath. "Perhaps. He pressed me as to Henri's father." She bit her lip.

"What did you tell him?"

"That he is not to discuss the subject with me again. Ever." She picked at the hem of her gown. "And that it is not his concern, as I do not care for that man."

Madame clicked her tongue. "You ask a lot of your lover, *mon amie. Mon Dieu*, if I requested the vicomte not discuss my former lovers, the young man would needs be quite silent."

Louisa spared her a pointed glance.

"He is quite curious, like all young men," Madame explained, shaking her head abruptly. "So, you have asked your Henry to trust you in this."

"I did not mention trust at all."

Madame crossed her arms over her ample chest and stared at Louisa. "You have asked him to trust that your heart is his alone, but you will not say yes to his proposal of marriage. You've borne another man's child, and you will not give him up." She raised her hand at Louisa's half-formed protest. "I understand your reasons, and I agree with them. But, Louisa, I am not a man. If someone slights me or someone I love, I take revenge with my brush, not my honour. It is also easy for me to love another child almost as much as my own."

"I did not ask him to accept Henri."

"Did you not?" Madame responded. "Think of all you have asked of him and all you know of him."

"Do you advise I should tell him my secret then?"

Madame Vignée gazed at the statuette of *Psyche Revived by Cupid's Kiss*. "I cannot tell you what to do, Louisa. You have asked him to become a certain kind of man. The kind who is so sure of you, he accepts your love on faith alone. This is no small request."

Louisa ran her hands over her clay model, stroking the slight curve over Psyche's belly that so few artists noticed. Psyche was pregnant when Cupid found her. Louisa was sure this was the case and she wanted this depicted in her painting.

"If he believes in your love for him, he will do as you wish. If you believe in his love for you…what will you do?"

Louisa remained silent, staring at her canvas. The General's godson was a beautiful man…his mouth curving up in a half-smile as he gazed down at Psyche, already moving to touch her body the way he'd always touched her heart. She blinked, unsure why tears seemed imminent at this moment.

"He agreed to give me time. I need time," she defended herself as best she could.

"You've known this Englishman all your life," Madame persisted.

"I need time," Louisa repeated, her voice fading.

"Are you attempting to convince me?" Madame asked sagely. "Or yourself?"

Louisa's tears threatened again. "I felt too much once before," she whispered. "I—I must not be a fool again. Not with Henri now. I cannot afford it."

"Not all men are like the one who deceived you," Madame spoke seriously. "Make no mistake, Louisa, the fault is on his side. The loss is on his side. Those who spend this Christmas with you—we are the gainers. Your Henry knows this, I am certain."

"Are you, Madame?" Louisa asked out loud. *I wish I were as certain as you.* "We have until Christmas," she said with a return of vigour.

"Christmas is mere days away," Madame pointed out as she donned her cloak and kissed Louisa on both cheeks. "*Bonsoir*, I will see you tomorrow as usual."

"*Bonsoir*, Madame."

Louisa rocked her son to sleep and returned to her work. She was in a rhythm now. Creating Henry's form on canvas seemed a further avowal of faith on her part. Faith in him, and in this growing warmth between them. As she leaned in to umber the outline of his rib cage, she had the strangest sensation he stood behind her, watching her work. She never allowed anyone to watch her work.

***

"We are taking a carriage ride to my sister's this day," Madame announced the next morning. "She has a nanny for her children, who is happy to take Henri while I attend to my Christmas errands. It is acceptable to his *maman*?"

"I should be ungrateful if it were not." Louisa smiled as she appeared from behind the screen, Henri securely fitted against her hip. Madame held out her arms, and the boy was delighted to go to her.

"Please allow your sister one of my works." Stepping to one side, she took up a smallish-framed piece depicting a vase of flowers beside a horn of fruits. She wrapped it with brown paper and quickly settled the string.

Madame Vignée nodded. "An excellent gift, *mon amie*. I shall not be late back with him. I wish to see more vermilion lips in my studio."

"Madame!" Louisa barely had a chance to protest before her tutor winked, leaving with Henri.

Since most of Louisa's neighbours believed the fiction of "Traversant's *la mademoiselle*," she decided it could do no harm to dispense with male garb for one day. It also made sense to meet Henry in feminine dress. Once attired in a demure grey gown, she tied on a painting apron and continued her next layer of work. When Henry's knock came, she did her best to subdue her heart's delighted leap. *No chance.*

"For Traversant." Henry bowed, offering a bouquet of Christmas roses to match his vermilion lips.

"The flower of Aphrodite—how fitting. Thank you, Henry." She kissed him softly, then arranged the roses in a vase beneath the light, feeling his gaze respond to the swish of her skirts as she positioned him on the divan.

The sitting filled almost an entire day, without the customary break for luncheon.

"I'm not hungry," Henry assured her, but by mid-afternoon Louisa needed to stop for her own health.

"While I appreciate your commitment to our work, I must take a moment or two, so please, rest yourself. I shall fetch your wine."

"I am quite capable of fetching wine if you'll tell me where to go," Henry replied.

Louisa bit her lips as she nodded towards the door. "The shared stillroom is opposite the studio doorway," she said, watching him intently. "There is no need for a key."

Henry donned his breeches, walked to the door, opened it—and could hardly pass out of the room. He looked back at Louisa, who didn't trouble to hide her grin.

"You knew I'd not fit through the doorway with these wings," he accused, his lips twitching.

Louisa laughed. "I confess I did." She laughed again and shook her head. "It's a poor artist who cannot judge the width of a doorway by eye. Monsieur Traversant's mademoiselle will only keep you a moment." She slipped out, returning a short time later with wine, bread, and a little cheese.

"I did not find the fruit," she explained. "It's rather haphazard, I'm afraid. I am not the only artist racing to meet the committee deadline for my admission piece."

"I daresay you're the only one strapping herself down for a chance of it," Henry commented.

Louisa shrugged. "I am surely not the first woman to attempt such a thing. Was there not a pharaoh at some stage?"

"Indeed," Henry agreed. "The ancients had far more concerns about placing a woman on their throne than the English."

Louisa shook her head.

"You do not agree?"

"I do not, but I am not in a humour to discuss it. My work is at a most interesting stage. I wish to complete the shading of Cupid's feathers before the light changes. The under layer will have dried by now. When you are ready?"

Henry assumed his position with an expression of chagrin. "Do you enjoy telling me what to do?"

"Less smiling please, as you were yesterday," Louisa commanded him, though she grinned in her turn. "It is an improvement from when we were children. You were always the leader, and I the younger, compelled to follow your orders. You were a leader of foolish underlings even then."

"Your memories do not match my recollections at all." Henry's laugh almost discomposed their work, but he regained his posture easily enough. Louisa let go a relieved breath, resolving there and then not to amuse her model during his sitting, which reminded her of something. She cleared her throat.

"*The Becoming of Love* is almost complete, dear Henry. I shan't need you to sit for me tomorrow." She smiled, though her heart gave a wobble, which she thought was very unfair. "You'll be free of those wings at last."

Henry flexed one powerful shoulder. "From divinity to mortality in one fell swoop," he quipped. "I've grown rather fond of them." He frowned. "Do you mean you'd rather I not come to see you?"

Louisa put down her brush, forcing herself to meet his gaze. "It is a distinct pleasure to see you in my studio," she answered honestly, wondering if the truth was always this difficult. *Is this truth?* She supposed it must be, because she did enjoy having him near her.

Would Henry still come to see her after today? If she agreed to his proposal, of course he would. Any betrothed man would use the advantage such an agreement gave him for easy admittance into female company. This was how women in her situation became so.

"Louisa?" Henry prompted.

"I beg your pardon, Henry. Is it your wish to call on me?"

"Call on you? Of course," he answered, sighing. "Do you doubt me?"

Louisa shook her head quickly. "It is not you I doubt." She cleared her throat.

Henry studied her a moment, nodding to himself. "What else is required for the work?"

"Only Cupid's eyes," she replied. "And Psyche's. I wish the lovers' eyes to convey a specific expression. Trust rebuilt, a greater love uncovered after their first pale effort."

"Is that so?" Henry smiled.

"It is my intent."

"The greatest lovers in history, each of whom made mistakes, reunited after some trials in a far more divine union. It sounds like the sort of proposal one could hardly refuse."

Louisa tried not to admire the smile in his fine blue gaze. "There is no need to smirk, Henry," but she adored the fire building in his eyes. "Then the only thing left to do is await the drying process and occasional touch-ups."

"Occasional touch-ups?" Henry repeated with an emphasis that had her tingling with anticipation. He drew her toward him, tasting her lips with his tongue.

"May we complete this tonight?" he asked, tracing patterns with his fingertips on the curve between her neck and shoulder.

Not entirely certain he meant her painting, Louisa groaned, trying her best to reply with sense. "Possibly, if I did not have Henri to tend to, our dinner time, and my study of the female form." Turning her head, she pressed her mouth against his and drew back. "It is very difficult to think when you're doing this."

"I am merely following artistic orders," Henry said, in between placing small, sensuous kisses along her jawline. "Occasional touch-ups are part of the–" he made his way down her throat, "formal process." He mumbled, his mouth nuzzling the sensitive skin above her bodice.

Louisa rewarded him with a long, low moan of pleasure that she cut short abruptly.

"Oh," she gasped, glancing at the clock. "Madame will be here soon."

"With Henri?"

"Yes." She smiled. "I confess, I do not like it when he is not with me."

"May I meet him today?"

Louisa pulled away from him and stared. "You wish to dine with us?" This time her shame had nothing to do with her circumstances and everything to do with the too-spare provisions to which she had access. Not to mention the meagre store of candles she'd been saving for Christmas. She couldn't bear any one's pity—especially not Henry's. Aware her silence occupied too long a space in their discourse, she tried to correct this.

"I do not think—" She swallowed. "I beg your pardon, Henry, but I cannot agree to engagements without Madame. This is her studio, you know."

"I understood her to be expelled," he replied. "In truth, it belongs to the Academy, does it not?"

Louisa stared. "Er, yes. How did you know?"

Henry shrugged. "Rumours, my dear. Come, allow me to see my namesake. I shall summon von Humboldt, who I am sure will be delighted, and we may enjoy a merry meal, excellent company, and witness the completion of a magnificent work of art."

His suggestion sounded so reasonable that Louisa hesitated to say no. Before she could formulate her thoughts, the bells for vespers rang out—which meant Madame was an hour past due with her charge.

Louisa clutched a palm to her breast. "Madame is *never* late," she explained. "Especially when she knows Henri's feeding program. Oh Henry, what if—"

Fear drove further words from her mind.

"Assuming the worst will not help." Henry took up his linen and shook his head at her as if that might stop such thoughts. "Where did they go today?"

His question gave Louisa pause. Breathing hard, she answered, "Her sister's, in Montmartre. Do you know the Rue du Mont-Cenis?"

"Wait here."

"I cannot!" She nearly shrieked. *Is he leaving me now?*

Henry reached for her hand, staring seriously into her eyes. "Allow me a moment to find a boy and send for von Humboldt. There is no part of this country he does not know, and his French is impeccable." He kissed her fingers. "Once he arrives, I shall send him after Madame. They are likely only delayed by the snow, but we shall await them here. If they arrive while you are absent, Henri may be further distressed, correct?"

"Yes." Louisa sighed, grateful beyond words that one of them remained collected enough to formulate a plan. "I will do as you suggest."

Henry lifted her hands to his lips and kissed them again. Throwing his caped coat over his dress, he left the studio.

The moment he was gone, Louisa sank onto her divan, her hands shaking and her heart panicking in her breast. Henry's calm command was helpful, but her mind did nothing but hammer *what if, what if, what if,* against the front of her skull until the only way to quiet such noise might include beating her head insensibly against the wall.

Henry returned with a large bottle full of dark liquid.

Once he'd brushed the snow from his shoulders, he searched for a corkscrew. "You'd best try this."

"Wine?" Louisa stared dubiously at the bottle.

"I rather doubt it." Henry found a way to remove the beeswax seal, cautiously sniffing the contents. "Brandy," he announced, wrinkling his nose and taking up a cup from one of the still life displays.

Louisa accepted her drink and sipped. "Will your friend take long?"

Henry shook his head. "There are few men I should call so reliable."

114

Chapter 13

An agonising half-hour slid by, and all Henry could do was hold Louisa's hands in his and pray. A sharp knock had him across the room in an instant, and von Humboldt bowed himself in. Henry was never more relieved to see a man in his life.

"It's good of you to come, baron."

"At your service, major and –?"

"I beg your pardon." Henry bowed as Louisa curtsied. "Baron von Humboldt, of Berlin, may I present Miss Beresford?"

"How do you do, Miss Beresford?" He bowed and lifted her hand, kissing the air above her knuckles.

"Good evening, baron. I believe you know my father?"

The baron raised his brow at Henry.

"The General," Henry explained.

"Ah!" von Humboldt nodded, further addressing Henry. "I understand my summons is urgent?"

Henry explained the situation as concisely as he could.

"Madame Vignée's sister? Yes, I know her. She too is an artist. In miniatures." Seeing Louisa's expression, he shook his head. "No matter, you wish me to journey to Montmartre and ascertain your friend's whereabouts?"

"Not merely Madame's whereabouts," Louisa hastened to add.

"She is travelling with a, well—" Henry's speech stumbled. "A babe."

"A what?" Von Humboldt looked as though he hoped he'd misheard.

"A baby," Louisa repeated. "She has charge of my son. He is not five months old, sir." She stared at both men, her eyes wide and stricken.

"I understand you, Miss Beresford." Von Humboldt took Louisa's shaking hand between his own, nodding sympathetically. He released her, shook Henry's hand, and opened the door. "I have *le hôtel*'s carriage outside," he assured them. "It's likely this weather delays them. Rest assured, Miss Beresford. I shall be back as soon as I am able. You are in excellent charge here." He nodded to Henry and left.

"Drink this." Henry poured out a little more liquor. For once, Louisa did not argue.

"Oh Henry, if anything should happen..." She shuddered.

"It is as von Humboldt says, dearest. A delay due to the snow. He is an excellent fellow." He looked at the grate. "Where is your coal?"

"There isn't any," Louisa admitted.

"Wait here." He knocked on the nearest doors without response. The third one he tried was answered by an odd fellow who seemed well in his cups. With a grizzled beard and a mere smattering of English, he stared at Henry.

"I'm come to purchase some of your stores." Henry proffered his coin and mimed the rest of his message. The old artist's eyes flew wide as he issued a command. A large, silent girl slid out from behind a screen without a stitch on. Wordlessly, she gathered coal, kindling, and a cloth bundle. Handing them to Henry with a mysterious smile, she took his coin and ushered him out. As he left, Henry caught sight of the marble piece for which the model had posed.

Returning to Louisa, he laid the fire and lit it while she untied the bundle. It turned out to hold apples, buns, and a generous wedge of cheese.

"Your neighbour seems kind." Henry tried for a wan smile. "The sculptor."

Louisa did not respond. The brandy seemed to be having its effect, though. She managed to swallow some cheese and fruit in between pacing the studio.

"Are you certain you'll not sit?" Henry suggested.

"I cannot."

"Then I shall walk with you." He paced beside her.

Louisa did smile then, sadly, wearily. "I am not the swooning type of woman, Henry. I cannot be still while Henri is not safe by me. Madame too," she added.

"Your distress will not do," he murmured, pressing a kiss to her temple.

A sudden inspiration came to him, and Henry lit the Sevres lamp, placing it beside the canvas. "Perhaps you might paint while we await news? You've the eyes to do." *Distraction.*

Louisa stood still at last, cocking her head to one side as she considered her canvas.

"The sooner I complete my work, the more time it shall have for drying." She shrugged, settling herself obediently by her easel before lifting the lamp high. "I must see your eyes, Henry."

"As you wish." He moved as close to the lamplight as he was able. Louisa leaned in to study the intricate twirls and flecks of irises and pupils. Henry breathed in relief as he stroked her hair and held her tight. "It will be all right, Louisa. Complete the work."

Nodding, she took up her brush, beginning with Cupid's eyes. After a few moments, Henry saw her shoulders drop.

"Thank you for suggesting this," she said once the first ultramarine was complete.

"It's best to keep busy," Henry agreed.

By the time Compline rang in, Louisa had completed her newest layers, and Henry was measuring out another glass of brandy and water. He watched her scraping down her palette and trying to rinse her brushes. Her hands shook so badly, he feared the splashes of turpentine.

"Allow me?" Henry swapped his drink for turpentine. "I believe I still recall how to care for an artist's brush." When he was done, he scraped down a fresh palette, hovering above the paint table. He squeezed out verdigris, yellow ochre, carbon black, and lead white, keeping one wary eye on Louisa's tense frame.

"Which is your brush for the finer lines?"

"The horsehair," Louisa whispered. "Why?"

"I have it." He took up the brush, loading it with a green colour thinned with poppy seed oil. "Do you remember the coldest Christmas we spent at Clayford?"

"Was that not the Christmas where the frost was so severe, there was no greenery to be had on the estate?" Louisa spoke slowly, as though her memories were further away than his.

"That's the one." Henry stepped back from the wall and turned to face her. "I believe we painted all the picture frames in the house." Beside him, Louisa's wall-mounted still life sported a fresh, ivy-leafed design. The execution was imperfect, but the sense of living greenery came through strongly.

"Papa refused us a penny for bought blooms," Louisa recalled, moving closer. "I did not know you still painted." She smiled faintly and shook her head. "You astound me, Henry. You are very good."

"Here." He held out the palette and brush, planting a kiss on her cheek. "Why not begin your Christmas decorations?"

Louisa leaned up and kissed his mouth. "Thank you," she replied, taking up the palette. Together, they moved around the little studio, outlining a trail of ivy along one frame, and a sprig of oak leaves in the corner of another. Each leg of the little dining table was soon covered with spruce leaves. Louisa even managed some holly on the frame of her silk screen. When she'd completed this, she turned to see more of Henry's work. He'd been busy for several moments, working quietly up a ladder in order to reach a ceiling cornice.

"Do take care, Henry."

"All done," he replied, jumping down. "I do hope I've captured the shape of the leaves accurately."

Louisa stood beside him, squinting upwards. "It looks like—"

"Yes?"

"Mistletoe. Is it mistletoe?" In answer, Henry kissed her tenderly on the mouth, feeling her smile. *At last.*

"It is," Henry replied, moving to mix another drink.

Louisa sipped it slowly but jumped when the door swung open.

"Steady!" Henry grabbed her slipping cup, thankfully rescuing it from oblivion, as Madame and von Humboldt crashed into the room.

"*Merci*, baron, *merci* indeed," Madame was saying as she kissed their new friend on both cheeks and turned to do the same for Louisa.

"Madame!" Louisa almost shrieked as her friend opened her cloak to reveal a sleeping, swaddled Henri warm and safe against her ample bosom.

Henry didn't think he'd ever forget Louisa's face in that moment: her relief, her joy, and her brightly shining love. The amber depths of her eyes glowing like fire, and her smile made his heart pound painfully against his ribs.

"Oh, my son!" Louisa kissed her friend, attempting to transfer her babe gently from Madame's embrace to her own. She must not have been gentle enough because as soon as she laid her son against her breast, he woke, attempting to nurse. Careful not to glance at Henry or von Humboldt, Louisa inclined her head and stepped behind the screen.

"I'll not keep any of you long," she assured them. "Henri missed his evening milk."

"I have seven younger siblings, Miss Beresford. I've seen many a child nurse," von Humboldt told her.

"That may be," Louisa replied from behind the screen, "but you've no need to see Henri do so."

Henry was gratified to hear him laugh. "Now, what has happened? Madame?"

"This vile weather," Madame told them. "We could not get back once the snowfall grew heavy. I had already sent the carriage back to the vicomte, and there wasn't a hack to be had. I could not think how to get you word, and I dared not walk through all that snow and wind with the *petit*."

"I thank you for keeping him safe, Madame," Louisa interjected.

"I had settled it with my sister that we must stay in some sort of makeshift bedding, when this wonderful man announced he was come after us, with a carriage in which to bring us home." Madame beamed at the baron.

"It is my honour to be of service to a talent such as yours, Madame Vignée." Von Humboldt bowed, while Madame's intelligent blue eyes swept over him, offering up her most gracious smile.

"I am so glad you are both safe." Louisa reappeared shortly after this.

"How is Henri?" Henry wanted to know.

"He was a little fractious, but the milk calmed him. He's settled in the cradle and seems quite well enough." She took her art teacher in an embrace and squeezed her hard.

"Without a doubt, those are the worst few hours I have spent in Paris to date. Madame, you are much loved, my dear friend."

"*Merci*, Louisa," the older woman replied, stepping away with something like moisture in her eyes. "Is anyone staying for coffee?"

"An inspired idea," Henry replied, and his friend agreed.

Madame assisted Louisa until they were all seated, each possessed of a warm coffee drink, liberally laced with brandy.

As they discussed the upcoming *Le Salon de Noël*, Henry saw Louisa excuse herself at one point, returning with a parcel she placed near the doorway. After sitting together above half an hour, the ladies appeared to weary.

The baron rose to a bow. "May I escort you home, Madame Vignée?"

"I thank you, baron, you are most kind."

"What do you say, Major? Ready to turn in?"

"Perhaps later."

Chapter 14

Louisa turned to stare at Henry. *Surely he can't mean to stay here?* It was bad enough that half the neighbourhood thought she was Traversant's mistress. There was no need to make such rumours worse.

The baron donned his hat, cloak, and gloves by the door. Louisa curtsied, offering the large parcel she'd prepared earlier. "One of my Christmas works," she told him. "I cannot thank you enough for your assistance this evening, baron."

"I am charmed, Miss Beresford." He bowed thrice and kissed her hand twice, quite overcome.

Madame took his arm as they braved the weather one more time, leaving Henry and Louisa together.

"What a charming man." Louisa stared after the baron with a smile on her face.

"He is," Henry agreed. "He is betrothed to a charming woman."

Louisa's smile widened. "I said he was charming, not that I loved him. Will that satisfy you?"

"Indeed not." Henry drew her close, staring into her eyes with unmistakable heat.

He leaned in to claim a kiss, drawing back before it could become much more. Louisa almost groaned.

"You cannot stay," she whispered.

"Of course not. I only wish to see Henri. May I?"

Louisa stared. "Of course, if you wish it."

"I do," Henry replied. "My little namesake has had a strange night."

Louisa led him to the little area behind the screen, where Henri lay snugly in his cradle. She watched Henry intently.

He stared down at her son, his face a mixed palette of wonder and delight. There was something else too—a kind of proud protectiveness she used to sometimes see in the General's eyes when she was young. Or in Madame's face when her student executed a particularly difficult technique rather well. *Pride, Henry is proud of my son.* She could have cried for joy and a measure of relief. She could have kissed him, loved him—loved him? *I already love him.*

Then what, oh what, was she waiting for? Louisa studied his handsome face.

"I almost prefer you out of your wings," she said.

"Almost?" Henry scowled and immediately took up his costume.

"What are you doing?"

"You do not wish a final study for your admission piece?" Henry asked. "I ought to mention that I may not be able to call for some days. I have business at the Embassy. Tedious, but necessary, and I do not want your artwork to suffer for it. Is it complete?"

"Er, yes. A few final touches remain."

"A last look, then." Henry managed his buckles himself before moving into the main space. He dragged the divan into its usual position and stood beside it, watching her. "Are you going to model Psyche, or does Cupid love alone?"

Louisa grinned. "Now there's a scandalous image."

Henry laughed softly, taking up his pose on the divan. Louisa slipped off her gown and underclothes, arranging herself beneath him. Henry's palm cupped one plump breast, as per Canova's statue. His thumb grazed her nipple, still tender from her child's mouth. Delicious tingles raced through her body as Louisa watched her lover's arousal form. Gazing up into Henry's eyes, she reached for his face, as Psyche reached for Cupid.

She examined their pose in the looking glass as minutely as she could before righting herself to study her canvas. Leaning in, she made a few minor touches to the wings and Psyche's eyes, echoing the gilded whites of the love god's feathered arrows.

"There," she sighed. "It is complete."

Henry divided the last of the brandy into two coffee cups. "A toast," he suggested. "To *The Becoming of Love*'s salon debut. I know one artistic gentleman who is ready to bid."

"You intend to bid?"

"I do, but I was referring to the baron. I saw him look at your easel while you ministered to Henri." Henry grinned. "He looked most impressed and that is no small compliment. He owns a gallery in Cologne, you know, and is considering sponsoring the Berlin Salon next year."

"He is *that* von Humboldt?" Louisa's delight increased. "I approve of him even more so."

"I daresay he approves of you too, though he believed he saw Traversant's works, not yours, my dear." Henry finished his drink and began gathering his clothes. "I did not tell him otherwise."

With his linen over his arm, he stood before her. "This will be your last opportunity to kiss a deity." He grinned, leaning towards her mouth.

"You are so good to me," Louisa sighed as he kissed her mouth in soft farewell.

"As are you, to everyone." She saw a powerful longing in Henry's eyes.

"Have you—do you wish to say yes to me, as yet?"

Louisa leaned against him, feeling the resonant rumble of his words in his chest. "You make it very difficult to refuse you."

Henry kissed the top of her head and stepped back, taking her hands. "Good," he replied quietly. "Then do not refuse." His smile was warmly genuine and gentle. His hands clasping hers were comfort and kindness, and her heart wanted to melt into his. To say yes in a whisper, a shout, a scream against his beautifully bare chest…

Yet she stood there smiling and silent, wishing she possessed such courage.

"Today has been our last day like this," she said instead, looking quizzically up at him. "I do not yet know what this means for you and me."

"It need mean nothing," Henry responded. "If you'll only say yes."

She leaned in, unbuckling Cupid's wings until a mere mortal stood before her again. *My Henry.* Turning to place the wings to one side, Louisa recalled Madame's words. *Was* she testing Henry? Putting him through some sort of trial to prove his worth, because Henri's father had abused her trust so completely? She did not like that idea at all. Henry—*her* Henry—had nothing whatsoever to do with Henri's father. The two men could not be less alike.

Besides, if this was love, then whatever she'd felt for Henri's father had been as painted roses to a true, blooming rose bush. There was a vast difference between real life and still life: both were beautiful creations, but only one offered permanence *and* momentum—the heart as well as the heartbeat. False flowers had longevity but no lasting relevance. Real roses... Louisa inhaled the fragrance of Henry's offering. Real roses offered beguiling scents and joyful truths, the kind of love that could be kindled, and rekindled, repeatedly. It was truly dizzying to be pursued with such determination, by a heart she knew to be forever true. Hadn't she known this man forever? *Haven't I loved him forever?*

Henry stood before her, waiting.

"I agree you're not a patient man," she said then, realising she did not mind this. Not from Henry.

He stepped back. "I beg your pardon, Louisa."

"Whatever for, dear Henry?"

"I do not mean to press you." He met her gaze, and she saw fear in his eyes for the briefest moment. *Fear?* From a man like this? Louisa was quite unexpectedly humbled.

"It is simply that—" He stopped. Louisa watched him bite his lip, exhale and shake his head, as though too many words remained within.

"What is it, Henry?"

"I cannot wait to make you mine, is all. To be with you forever." His smile was so many shades of beautiful...kindness, admiration, desire, and—Louisa gasped—*love*. It was there, she recognised it, burning so intensely that she turned away, turned her back, could not look love in the face for very long, in case she could not escape its gaze within herself. But why would she want to? In that moment, she knew her fear, and pushed it away. *I need not fear him.*

She knew this man's heart as well as her own. She trusted him, respected him, admired him. Loved him.

Dear God, how I love my Henry.

"Yes, Henry," she said finally. "Yes, I will marry you."

"Oh, Louisa." Henry's arms came around her from behind, hugging her tightly to him, his cock pressing against her buttocks as he kissed the back of her neck.

It was all he could do to find her, touching her softness until she moaned his name again. He buried his mouth in the curve of her shoulder, kissing her with a thoroughness that had her leaning back, pulling him against her as he positioned himself behind, splaying her legs farther apart to take him. His hands cupped her breasts as his thumbs stroked hard, swollen nipples and his cock teased her curls. Louisa's legs shook and her body sang with pleasure as he stroked himself against her, tasting the sensitive skin at her temple with his lips and tongue. Her tingles became throbs and she was thrusting backwards into him, pushing her hips between his palms. She took her rhythm from his steady strokes, and his heated words, as he moved her to pleasure. She cried out and shook and shook again until she heard him gasp.

"I cannot, Louisa, I can't wait." He let out a groan, collapsing against her shoulders to bead tiny kisses along her spine.

"If this is how you accept my proposals, you ought to know I intend to propose to you every night from now on." He was still panting. "How I love you, Louisa."

She felt the strength of his embrace and uttered a small, satisfied moan of joy. "I love you, Henry."

He hugged her tight and helped her dress again before arranging his own. "This will be a Christmas to remember," he whispered against her ear as he kissed her good night. Louisa shivered with delight and kissed him back, wondering why on earth she'd been afraid at all.

"I'll see you for Christmas Eve," she reminded him. "When Cupid and Psyche are reunited on canvas."

"Not merely on canvas, my love." Henry pressed a firm kiss to her lips and left.

Chapter 15

Louisa awaited the final few days before Christmas with a confusion of pride, trepidation, and some little shyness. She rose predawn to tend to Henri and ready her artwork for Traversant's admission presentation, mentally listing the tints she required for touch-ups. She may have spent unnecessary moments staring into Cupid's eyes. *Henry's eyes*, smiling to herself as she rocked her babe gently, watching him feed.

"You're a good boy, Henri." She kissed his little hairless scalp and sat him against her shoulder, rubbing his back.

The bells rang out for matins, and Louisa sighed. She'd not seen Henry for several days, and though he'd explained this, her twinges of unease remained. She comforted herself with thoughts of the last time they'd been together. Her body heated instantly. She could hardly wait to become his wife. To love and be loved the way he'd shown her. It was something she'd never dreamed possible, and he had made this real for her. She was grateful—more than that, she loved him and wanted, so badly, to show him how much.

"Perhaps we may bid *au revoir* to Monsieur Traversant before the new year," she said to her son, kissing the top of his head one more time.

"Now," she told him, "lie down while Mama dresses." Placing her babe on his back on an old shawl, she stepped behind the screen to make up her bed and become Monsieur Traversant.

A plaintive wail brought her back around in a hurry. She scooped up her little son in surprise.

"Did you turn over? You clever little lad, your *Tante Vignée* will be so proud of you." She looked around for a more secure place for her child. "If you're going to start navigating your way so smartly, Henri, we'd best give this some thought." Louisa returned to her dress, taking her son with her, and placing him on the soft bed. She breathed a sigh of relief as he sucked on his fingers, seemingly content to stare back at his mama.

"*Bonjour*," Madame announced as she slipped into the room. "How is my *petit* this day?"

"Moving on his own." Louisa brought him out from behind the screen. "A strong one, our lad." She watched as Madame clapped Henri's hands for him, a game guaranteed to make him giggle.

"I shall take extra care," Madame said, gathering up Henri and her basket. "We will return later today, *oui*? You will celebrate with your betrothed before we dine?"

Louisa shook her head. "Henry remains ensconced at the Embassy, Madame. Besides, I do not wish to celebrate without you. You are as much a part of this work as Henry. You did engage his sitting."

"And very rewarding it has been," Madame replied. "You agreed to wed this man you love so deeply. I assure you he wishes to drink champagne and make love with you tonight. I may find excellent company for Henri among my sister's children. One night's absence from the vicomte's bed will do him no harm." She looked down to sigh pleasingly at her décolletage.

"In truth, it may do him good. He speaks of the other models in a way I do not like." She scowled for a moment but smiled when Henri took the lace frill of her bonnet in his chubby little fist.

"Lace, young man? What taste you have, sir!" Delighted with her charge, the artist placed her basket over her arm and bustled out.

By the time Madame and Henri arrived home, Louisa's work was dry enough to present.

"There," she lifted her cloth carefully upward, "*il est fini*, Madame."

"Is it ready for viewing?"

Louisa shrugged lightly. "I do hope so."

Madame stepped behind the easel and studied the canvas for a long time.

Louisa fidgeted and tried not to hold her breath. After what seemed an age, she could bear it no longer.

"Well, Madame? Will it do?"

Madame's gaze moved between the cast of Canova's statue and the erotically charged work on the canvas. "It is wonderful, *mon amie*," she pronounced at last, as though uttering a benediction. "*The*

Becoming of Love is a true work of art. You have not signed it," Madame pointed out. "Traversant must sign his work."

Louisa hesitated. "I understand it, Madame, but what then?"

"They will not expel you, Louisa. Your work is simply too good. *Mon Dieu*, if I had such vision at your age, I would not now be reduced to charming commissions out of too-dull Bourbonnes."

"You believe I may reveal myself once I am admitted, and they will accept it?"

Madame shrugged. "No one knows what the future brings, *mon cher*, and you are too brave to live your whole life in fear of this."

Louisa tossed her auburn curls and nodded. "I thank you, Madame." Leaning forward, she made Traversant's mark with a slight flourish and turned away.

Quietly, she set about completing the formalities for entering *Le Salon de Noël* and applying to *l'Académie*. Madame looked over her papers, advising few changes, and Louisa nodded, listening. Both popped behind the screen several times to check on the babe. Neither mentioned Henry: not then, and not when Madame began to nod in her seat so heavily that Louisa put her to bed behind the screen, while settling herself on the divan with too few blankets and a heavily unhappy heart.

She listed her blessings before she slept, counting her good friend, her son, and her ability to paint among her greatest. She chose not to mention other acquaintances. *Betrothal or no, if I hear nothing by Christmas Eve, I shall give him up forever*, was her last thought before sleep took her.

***

Rising to the call of matins the next day, the first thing Louisa did was check her work. The paint was slow to dry in this damp weather, but she had much to occupy her. After feeding Henri, she pulled back the covering from the mirror and returned to her larger canvas. Dropping her garments in a circular heap around her child, she trusted to Henri's curiosity as she once again absorbed herself in her study of the female form. Staring awhile at the sketch she'd made too quickly of the *Dresden Venus*, Louisa nodded slightly. She continued working the oil into her vermilion and umber until she'd achieved the same sheen of auburn hair in her likeness, as in herself.

As the sun rose higher, lighting her work via the oculus windows, she nodded in satisfaction and put down her tools.

Wrapping her son and herself up as warmly as possible, Louisa sallied out into the snow-bound streets in search of raisins, chocolate, and whatever other fare she might obtain for Christmas. With luck, one or two of Traversant's paintings may sell between now and the quarter day. At this time of year, Parisienne shopkeepers were inclined to be generous, particularly since the post-war mood was buoyant.

"Will we see you at *Le Salon de Noël*, mademoiselle?" the grocer asked as he handed over her purchases.

"*Oui*, monsieur."

"*Le Salon de Noël* is meant for good Christians, not little English *putes*," said the old lacemaker. Removing her sodden cheroot, she aimed a spit at Louisa. Louisa jumped back, her scorching cheeks adding to her worsening frame of mind. She needn't have despaired.

"*Assez! Sors.*" The grocer chased the old woman through the door with forceful hands. "Do not listen to such a sour old woman." He bowed. "You are welcome any time, mademoiselle, and especially at Christmas." His smile was kind as he nodded at Henri.

"Such a fine *bébé*." He nodded at her, slipping in more woollen skeins as he wrapped the rest of her goods. "A child's first Christmas must always be a celebration, and this year—no war." The grocer beamed at Louisa and the world in delighted munificence.

Louisa curtsied and tried to smile. "I thank you for your kindness, monsieur," she replied. "I hope to see you before the new year."

The revulsion on the lacemaker's face followed her onto the street, the freezing wind seeming to mock her with the old woman's word. *Pute…whore.* Louisa shuddered, hurrying through her remaining errands as she stowed her last few purchases in her basket. She doubted she'd ever get used to being seen as an immoral oddity, and she was not sorry to be back in her apartments and out of the cold in very short order.

By the time she settled her babe at her breast again, she was over her shock and ready to be cross. Placing her son as securely as she was able on an old woollen shawl, she laid all her parcels out one by one, taking up the nuts and her mortar and pestle. "The pudding must come first, Henri."

She found enough rum to leave a small pudding bagged and hung before beginning her holiday confectionary. The process took most of the afternoon. When Louisa dropped into bed later that night, exhausted and pleased with her day's activities, she barely had time to wonder what had become of Henry. Her eye caught the painted mistletoe glimmering in the moonlight. She scowled as her pangs of unease doubled.

The next day was Christmas Eve. Henry was to arrive before Traversant's admission presentation so they might dine together. Louisa painted in the morning and spent the afternoon creating her Christmas sweets, stirring carefully before adding in the colours she could afford. The process was not unlike painting. Smiling, she made up the parcels of *dragée* for her fellow artists and her friend the grocer. His kindness in extending her some credit allowed them to have a small fire, and Henri was as cosy as possible in this draughty old palace. As she set the newest batch of sweets to dry, the door opened to admit Madame, wearing what appeared to be at least two cloaks. Her eyes lit up when she saw the fire.

"Ah, this is my miracle," her teacher sighed as she divested herself of several layers, inching closer to the warmth. "Is there any felicity greater than a warm fire at Christmas?" She shook out her cloaks, and Louisa noticed the flakes dissolving in the heat.

"Is it snowing again, Madame?"

"*Oui, mon amie*. The *Rue de Rivoli* is becoming impa xssable. We must hope it improves by tonight."

"That's not likely, is it? The weather in December worsens. It does not lighten."

Her art tutor shrugged. "This may be true, but we still hope. If the visitors attending our exhibit cannot travel to Paris, our first *Le Salon de Noël* since *la terreur* will make an extremely poor showing indeed." She frowned. "I, for one, am counting on some wealthy Parisiennes to purchase from me. I—all the artists of Paris—need *Le Salon de Noël* to be a success."

Louisa nodded emphatically.

Madame looked closely at *The Becoming of Love*, narrowing her eyes. "This is ready for submission."

"*Oui*." Louisa kept her eyes on the small calico bags she was stitching.

"I wish to ask—" Madame began.

Louisa tensed visibly. *I am not ready to speak of Henry.*

"—if you might accompany me to Midnight Mass tonight?"

Louisa relaxed. "You know I am not Catholic, Madame."

"I do not wish to attend this night alone," her friend said in a low voice. Louisa looked up and reached out, squeezing Madame's hand.

"You shall not grieve your family alone. I shall attend by your side, and willingly, though I do not know the service."

Madame smiled at her, the blue eyes soft for once. "*Merci.* The order of service is of little matter. I shall not be thinking of that. I prefer instead to remember my dear Charles, and Louis, and my own tiny Henri."

The gentleness in her blue eyes reminded Louisa so forcibly of Henry that she turned deliberately away. Later that night, however, with Henri swaddled securely beneath her cape and stepping carefully through the icy streets, Louisa slipped her arm through Madame's and they made their way to Saint-Pierre de Montmartre. As they reached the lower part of the steps, they spied a familiar face.

"Baron von Humboldt." Madame curtsied and tugged at Louisa, who followed a moment later, using an arm to support Henri's weight.

"Merry Christmas, ladies." The baron bowed. "Do you attend midnight mass?"

"Indeed," Madame spoke for both of them. "It is too good of Miss Beresford to accompany me. She is not a Catholic, you know."

The baron immediately offered his arm. "Then, as I attend the services as well, may I escort you, Madame?"

Madame agreed at once. "I thank you. I am certain Miss Beresford would rather keep the little one indoors."

Louisa did not attempt to deny this, nor could she pretend to be sorry for it. She could only be grateful for the understanding of both her friends this night. Turning immediately, she hurried back along the route she'd already walked, warmed from the exercise, and from the heaviness of her son beneath her cape. She'd far rather return to her art. With any luck, perhaps she'd find another quart of that vile brandy in the stillroom—and drink it.

Louisa couldn't resist looking into the exhibition rooms as she hurried past. The porters had left for the evening, presumably to attend the midnight mass themselves. Henry was well overdue, and she refused to think of him any further. Laying Henri in his cradle, she changed into Traversant's clothes and stepped across the hall to examine the stillroom. *Empty*, but then, Louisa was not the only one accessing these stores to provide a Christmas feast.

Never mind. She had a better idea. As she was already attired accordingly, Louisa determined to peep into the deserted *Grande Gallerie* for a last viewing of her admission piece. Gathering a brush and her smaller touch-up palette, she made her way downstairs with the aid of one of her preciously reserved candles. She met no one. *What did you think? That a dashing English major would attend you as he said he would?* When would she learn not to be taken in by divine dark curls and a heart-melting smile?

"Not to mention his ultramarine blue eyes," she scoffed under her breath, pushing further thoughts of Henry firmly from her mind. "Barely a half-hour remains, and I've artwork to check." *He is not coming.*

It took her some time to locate her piece. When she did find it, Louisa could not resist a warm glow of pleasure. *The Becoming of Love* hung in a central position, opposite the main doorway, and likely one of the first pieces to catch the eye of those visiting *Le Salon de Noël* during the holiday. It was not the largest work, but it stood out. Both the powerful subject and her strength of execution were undeniable.

Louisa narrowed her eyes, noting a few minor adjustments she'd prefer to make. She was a little short of the height she needed, but an obliging porter had left a wheeled stepladder by a wall. With great care—and grateful her skirts no longer hampered her—Louisa set her candle aside and moved the ladder into position.

Taking up her palette, brush, and candle, Louisa balanced herself precariously. She sighed, touching up more of the finer details for which Traversant's work was becoming known. So engrossed was she that she barely noticed the final chimes heralding midnight, the first hour of Christmas Day—and the end of all her hopes for Henry. Only the shifting sunlight caused Louisa to look away from her work. It was getting on towards dawn. Her gut gave a sickening lurch, and she fought to steady herself. *Henry is not coming.*

Struggling to lay down her brush without marring nearby canvases, Louisa sank to the floor beside the ladder. Strangely, she did not cry. A part of her acknowledged an absurd sense of relief—

she need not believe in this man again. *Or in any?* Staring accusingly up at the image of Henry-Cupid, Louisa wondered if she'd asked too much.

"Cupid," she scolded aloud, "you and I are guilty of errors in judgment." She touched her brush to her palette, where only vermilion and ultramarine blue remained. "Asking your lover to be satisfied with ignorance is a fool's errand," she muttered to the painted deity. If the obedient Psyche could not manage this, why would a mortal man? *Why would Henry?*

"Madame tried to tell me so." She stared at her image of the two deathless lovers, her gaze hovering over the slight curve at Psyche's belly. "A dream, no doubt. Nothing but a foolish dream for a woman like me," she spoke aloud to her art.

After all his assurances of reliability, his declared excitement about her art—about *her*—Louisa's disappointment was heavier than the moment she realised Henri's father no longer wished to know her. *He has what he wanted of me, so why should he return? Why should he stay?* Why, indeed?

Louisa stared at her boots: Traversant's boots. Three of his other pieces hung for viewing—in prime places, not skied at all. Looking around *Le Salon de Noël*, she saw some few works signed by members of *l'Académie*'s admissions committee. What had she created with this deception? In some strange, disjointed way, Traversant seemed another man who robbed Louisa of herself. She stood, staring up at her hard work.

"I've had *quite* enough of Monsieur Traversant," she said loudly to Cupid and Psyche. Gathering her palette and brush, Louisa blew out the remains of her candle and dashed upstairs. After seeing Henri into his warmest garb, she changed into a velvet gown and gathered him to her. Donning her shawl and swinging an old reticule of Madame's over her wrist, Louisa returned to the as-yet-unpopulated exhibition, positioning herself opposite *The Becoming of Love* once more. Wheeling the little ladder back in place, she climbed up and took a deep breath, closing her eyes in momentary prayer.

Painting out Traversant's mark, Louisa repaired the canvas as best she could. Bending to the opposite corner, she etched her initials in a shade of vermilion that precisely matched her lips. Placing one hand beneath her babe, she stepped slowly down the ladder and stood back, studying the first exhibited work signed by *her*. *The*

Becoming of Love glowed just as brilliantly, the red initials complementing her lovers' lips.

It was likely she'd given up *l'Académie*, but this seemed far better than giving up herself. Staring back at Henry-Cupid, Louisa did her best to create a sense of finality. For the first time since she'd picked up a brush, she nearly regretted her skill. Her god of love resembled Henry in every inch. Glancing at her styled drapery, she smiled sadly. *Every* inch.

"I am rather good, you know," she said to the perfection of Henry's face. Ignoring the painful pangs of her battered heart, she turned determinedly away from Henry's—*Cupid's*—beautiful visage to indulge in her favourite kind of beauty.

Releasing a deep breath and straightening her stance, she walked the rooms of *le Louvre* with soft, deliberate steps, taking time to stop and absorb the creations of her fellow artists. *This is where my soul lies. This is where I come to heal.*

Pausing for a long while before a family tableau, she smiled in earnest. She did not need to read the description to know this was one of Madame's—indeed it showed Madame, her late husband the art agent, and their two boys; all lost to her friend now. Louisa's understanding of loss was different to her teacher's but no less piercing.

She walked on, pausing before a piece that, despite all the attendant scandal (or perhaps because of it), was expected to act as a successful draw for *Le Salon de Noël*. Louisa gazed again at Madame's work. "*La Madone et l'enfant*," read the description. Even here, Louisa remained unnamed. She stared at the image of herself and her Henri for a very long time, noting the "indelicate" display of teeth and the softly joyous expression in her eyes as she ministered to her son. She sighed then, a sense of harmony and belonging washing through her. Her spirits lifted a fraction. *Madame is right. Art* is *truth. It is also beauty, and solace, and peace.*

Right now, art is all I have.

A movement beneath her cloak seemed indignant. *Art and Henri.*

The pain hit her then—the deep dark pain of carbon black without a hint of ivory light. Looking down at her hands, Louisa shook and gulped, shrinking into herself. *I should have known…* The refrain echoed through her mind over and over until her head began to nod, and the repetitive sounds beat against her brain like *batteurs*

in battle. It steadied her somewhat, knowing she was alone in this—
again. Her child shifted against her in sympathy. *Not quite alone.*
Shaking herself, she pushed her shoulders back, steadying her
thoughts.

*I will return to my work. I will complete my study of the female
form. I will submit it as my reception piece, and it will sell.* She
completed a quick calculation in her head. *I shall not spend another
moment of my time on one who does not think of me, or Henri. This
is my son's first Christmas, and I shall make it wonderful.*

Chapter 16

Winter sunbeams stole through the *Grande Gallerie*, illuminating the gold-flecked paint in Madame's *Madonna and Child*. Louisa stood before her teacher's vision, the reassuring weight of her son heavy against her body. Did Madame truly see her as something divine? Louisa sighed…*if only*.

"It's a handsome piece," a deep voice said beside her. "Near the best I've seen."

Louisa turned slowly to face him. "Henry." She barely curtsied, turning to leave, determined not to remain here for one more moment. That might be all it took to fling herself into his arms, and she *would not*.

He caught her arm.

Louisa looked down, her gaze fixed below. "Let me go, Henry."

Henry did not listen. He did not move from his position. "What is it?" he asked urgently. "Louisa, what's wrong?"

"You—you did not come to me." She stared around for a pillar, or a wall, or even a paintbrush—something solid that she might grasp for support. The only thing within reach was Henry's strong, steady arm. She shuddered beneath his hold. *The gods play cruel tricks*.

"I take it you didn't receive my note?" The tightness in his voice softened too quickly, sounding like a plea.

Louisa shrugged as though her shoulders were heavy stone, seeking refuge in silence. Her resolve wavered. *Henry deserves a hearing*.

"Louisa, truly, I beg your forgiveness. My Embassy work took longer than anticipated. The politics are delicate, and I couldn't get away so I sent a note. I am beginning to feel the continental post owes me a debt for the blight it brings to my affairs."

Louisa felt his eyes on her, watching for her smile. "I'll not allow you to charm me again. I-I would prefer to go now."

His voice stayed high and tight, full of fear. "You truly wish to go? You do not trust this love of ours?"

"No," she whispered, unwilling to speak such a lie too loudly. "Do you?"

"Yes," Henry said softly, turning her to face him. "Please know I did not intend to hurt you. I would never—" He swallowed, and his voice shook. "I could not hurt you intentionally, dearest. Love is full of mistakes, Louisa, but need they ruin all?" She heard a choking sound, as though he cried. *Impossible.*

"I do not know what to do," she mouthed.

Henry reached for her hands. Louisa flinched, but he wasn't finished.

"What must be done is this: I must beg your pardon, and you must forgive me, because—" He paused, and the choking sound came again. His voice thickened and heaved. "Because I will not give you up. I love you."

Louisa was safer if she stared at the floor. *Safe, safer, safest*...there was something to be said for safest. There was something more to be said for the warmth of his hands holding hers. He trembled, and her resolve shook.

"Will you not look at me, dearest?"

Louisa shook her head again, keeping her lips pressed tightly closed and her eyes dry. *Safer.* Something warm and wet landed on her wrist. A single teardrop beaded like a pearl.

"I love you," he said again, and her resolve splintered like dried-out clay.

"I'd given you up," she admitted, her voice firmer now. "I-I thought you'd gone."

"Not without you." He reached for her waist and pulled her closer. "Not this time. Not ever again, my love." Tucking his finger beneath her chin, he tipped up her face, kissing her lightly.

Kissing isn't safe. Louisa ignored this sound advice, drawing back from his mouth a fraction too late. "What do you mean?" she whispered, desperately wishing to return to his kisses.

"Louisa, I asked you to be my wife." He kissed her again, softly, and drew back. "It was no idle thought. Do you truly believe—" He swallowed. "Do you think so poorly of me?"

"I-I did not want to believe so, Henry. Truly, I did not. You are the best man I've ever known. I *did* consider that perhaps you'd changed your mind. I bear you no ill will for this. It is no easy burden to take up with a woman like me."

"There *is* no other woman like you. Not for me." Henry tightened his arms around her waist. "You asked me to trust you." He pressed a kiss to her brow. "Will you trust *me* now?" he said gently. "After all, you know me better than anyone else."

She saw his eyes then. His divine blue eyes, wet and soft, so overflowing with love and fear, she could not bear it. Louisa buried her head against his chest, hugging him as tightly as she could. She looked up at his soft grunt.

"What is it, Henry?"

"Never mind," he whispered, his lips close beside her ear. "Where is Henri?"

"Swaddled beneath my cape."

"Then come with me now."

Good lord, he sounded commanding when he needed to. Louisa had no trouble believing men followed Henry into battle.

"Come with you? Now? It is barely light on Christmas Day." *Was he mad?*

"I'm not mad," Henry answered her.

"I spoke it aloud?" Oh God, her cheeks burned.

"You did." His eyes warmed as he looked down at her. "This is not madness, Louisa. This is love. *Our* love, and the sooner you learn to trust this, the better. We'll begin immediately—so, come." He took her hand in his, guiding her to the street.

"It is far too cold to be out…why—" She stared up into the truly dark day. "There's *snow*." She slipped in her ill-suited boots, but Henry's arm was beneath hers in a moment, his other waving towards a coachman parked a short way down the street.

At his signal, the carriage drew up beside them. A smart man jumped down and dropped the steps for her.

"Step in, do," Henry assured her. "We'd best get a move on before the roads worsen."

"Are we taking a journey?" Louisa climbed in. She'd barely unbuttoned her cape before noticing she shared this heavenly warm compartment with a man she'd not met before.

"Miss Beresford." The man put out his hand.

"Good morning, er—"

"Merry Christmas," Henry said, addressing them both with a handshake, though he continued to hold Louisa's, stroking her wrist gently through her glove. "This is Mr Briscall, an old friend of mine. He's stationed at the British Embassy," Henry explained. "I could hardly allow him to spend Christmas alone." He smiled mysteriously at her. "Try the hot box, both of you."

Louisa noticed that the carriage was the kind with hot bricks. She placed her feet over the metal box with a sigh. Their companion did the same.

"If your intent is to pique my curiosity, it is most effectively done." Louisa relaxed somewhat now she was warm again. With Henry again—she turned to him with raised brows. "I'll not speak another word until someone explains this conspiracy."

Henry's friend smiled. "You are a fortunate man, Musgrave."

Henry grinned in response. "I am aware."

His grin was profoundly irritating to Louisa. The most annoying thing about Henry was how handsome he was, how exciting—*and how much I love him*, she admitted, watching his warm blue eyes.

Henri woke and decided to make himself heard. "I beg your pardon." Louisa smiled at the gentlemen as she adjusted her cape until her son peeped out at the rest of them with his usual gummy grin. He seemed content enough to stare at the flurrying flakes beyond the window, the motion of the carriage soothing him.

"We are not travelling far," Henry assured her. "Just to Montmartre."

"Why?" Louisa asked, noticing that Briscall did not look the least bit surprised.

"You'll see." Henry patted her hand.

Louisa had never wanted to slap a man more. "You are enjoying this far too much."

Henry merely smiled in response. "It *is* Christmas," he reminded her. "A day made for surprises."

The carriage slowed at that moment, and Louisa found herself helped down by Mr Briscall. Henry took charge of Henri before handing him to the smart coachman. "Do you think you can manage this fellow, Baker?"

The man bounced Henri effectively, receiving a gurgling giggle in response. "I've nine of my own, Major. Leave this to me."

He walked beside them, and Louisa was not sorry to be relieved of the weight of her son.

"You are excellent with him, Mr Baker. I thank you."

The older man smiled. "Mrs Baker is nurse to many ladies of quality," he replied. "Not but that she didn't nurse all our nine herself as well. You've a fine lad here."

It's as well Louisa had Baker's assistance. What with the snow and churned-up path, the climb to the butte was not for the faint-hearted. She was warmed enough by the time she crested the hill and turned, gazing down upon a snow-covered Paris.

"A beautiful city," she sighed, turning to Henry. "If this is why you've brought me here, I approve. Shall we watch the sun rise?"

To Louisa's surprise, it was Briscall who responded. "If you'll follow me, Miss Beresford?"

He led their party alongside the abbey ruins and into *L'Église sur la Butte*. Once in sight of the sacristy, Louisa's hand flew to her mouth. "Oh!"

Candles sat on every available surface of the old stone altar. There, in the pews, stood Madame and their friend the baron, with a petite blonde woman who, by the way he looked at her and she at him, could only be his lady Rebecca. Dozens of candles illuminated the gloom as though Madame herself had painted the scene. If it were not for the flickering of hundreds of small flames, Louisa might think it a still life.

Henri made a few sounds, and she reached for him. Once she'd settled her son at her hip, she gazed up at her Henry in amazement. "However did you find so many candles?" was her first question.

Henry laughed. "It's true we seem to have bought up the city's entire store, but can you blame me?"

"Whatever for?" Louisa stared at him.

"For our wedding day, my love." He smiled as Briscall took his place before them, smoothing the pages of a small book drawn from beneath his caped officer's coat. "This is the *Reverend* Samuel Briscall, chaplain to His Majesty's forces currently serving in France. Did I not say?"

Louisa shook her head slowly. "You did not." She turned and curtsied to the chaplain. "Candles and a minister." She smiled. "You astound me, Henry."

Their companion cleared his throat. "It's after eight, Major. Shall we begin?" Addressing himself to Louisa, he explained, "We've very little time, Miss Beresford. We are not the only people wishing to make use of our Church on the Hill this Christmas day."

Madame stepped forward to take Henri in her arms, using the opportunity to squeeze Louisa's hand and kiss her on both cheeks. "*Joyeux Noël, mon amie.* You deserve such love as this, and so much more."

"Wilt thou have this woman to be thy wedded wife? Wilt thou love her, comfort her, honour and keep her, in sickness and in health; and, forsaking all others, keep thee only unto her, so long as ye both shall live?" the Reverend Briscall intoned, smiling at them both.

"I will," Louisa replied slowly.

Beside her, Henry shook with silent laughter. "I believe he's speaking to me," he whispered.

Louisa almost shut her eyes in embarrassment—but she didn't. She did not want to miss a moment of her wedding day. Her Christmas day. Henri's first, and her first with both Henri and Henry together. All that was missing was—

"Who giveth this woman to be married to this man?"

"I do," came a voice Louisa never thought to hear again. She spun around at the sound of the door banging shut, staring as the General shook the snow from his caped coat and swept up the aisle to stand beside his daughter, at last.

"A moment, sir," he addressed the chaplain briefly.

Reverend Briscall nodded. "I would not delay," he replied, indicating a small group of men entering the bell tower.

"Understood," the General replied before turning to Louisa. "I should never have sent you away, child." Taking her right hand in his, her father looked into her face. "Can you ever forgive me?"

"Oh Papa." She smiled through her brimming tears. "I understood you to be in Vienna."

"May we defer such explanation til we complete the nuptials, hmm?" Their vigilant guide glanced again towards the church doors.

"I beg your pardon, Reverend." The General placed Louisa's hand in the minister's and stood back in his place. "Do go on, sir."

Briscall placed Louisa's hand in Henry's and repeated his questions for Louisa this time.

"I will," she replied stoutly, feeling Henry's fingers gripping hers tightly. *My Henry.*

"I, Henry George Musgrave, take thee, Louisa Jane, to be my wedded wife—"

The rest of the words were lost in a swirl of sensations as Louisa looked into Henry's face and saw his faith in her. She hardly heard his promise "to love and to cherish." He'd already done so, was doing so in this moment—and he'd always done so. Louisa finally trusted him to continue loving her.

"—and thereto I plight thee my troth," Henry repeated after Briscall.

Louisa spoke the words along with him, unable to wait for her turn.

"Do you have—" but before Briscall could finish, Henry placed a pretty silver band on the prayer book, then took Louisa's other hand in his, turning her to face him.

Glancing up into Henry's eyes, she knew he saw the urgency in her face. Saw it, understood it, and responded to her rush to become his. Those eyes of his darkened, and Louisa had to remind herself very firmly that they stood in a house of God.

"With this ring, I thee wed, with my body I thee worship," Henry began, repeating after Briscall. A moment after the reverend's blessing, Henry slipped the band over her fourth finger and completed his vow.

Louisa held her breath as their friend concluded with his announcement that they were "—man and wife together."

Shooing them all out past the tabernacle, their clerical friend stood beside them, gazing towards the artistry that was Paris at Christmastime. After a moment, he offered his hand to Henry.

"Merry Christmas, Major, and my sincerest congratulations." Turning to the General, he offered a salute. "Congratulations, General." The chaplain moved on to pay his respects to Madame, the baron, and his lady Rebecca

Louisa watched her papa return the reverend's salute before approaching her. "You've been much missed," he replied, casting curious looks at his grandson. "I must beg your pardon that our acquaintance suffered interruption from such a stubborn old fool." Taking Louisa's hand in his, the General raised it to his lips. "I couldn't be prouder, Louisa," he insisted. "Truly."

Louisa looked him in the eye. "Papa, if this is about returning to Clayford—"

"It is not," her father replied, glancing again at Henri. "Though perhaps it would be wise to spend Christmastide elsewhere."

"My work," Louisa began, but Henry stood by her side.

"As I wrote you, sir, Louisa's work is here. However, the baron invites us to spend Christmastide in Berlin. As his wedding is to be held shortly, this is an excellent opportunity for our wives to become acquainted." He paused, turning to Louisa. "That is if you wish it?"

Louisa stared at him. "The baron wishes me to make his lady's acquaintance?"

"More than this, I believe." Henry indicated the close conversation of Madame, the baron, and his lady Rebecca. "He is keen to sponsor a salon of his own and wishes to engage you and your tutor."

"He will exhibit my work?" Louisa had to say the words aloud to make them real. "*My* work, not Traversant's?"

"He finds *The Becoming of Love* far superior to anything created by Traversant," Henry answered with a warm smile seemingly reserved for her. "His critique of art improves all the time."

"You have done all this? For me?"

"No, Louisa, *you* have done this. Your work is too good to be hidden behind a false persona." He took her hands in his and stared down at her, heated pride and admiration shining in his eyes. "Step into the light, my wife, my dearest, my heart. Merry Christmas, Louisa."

Her eyes would not focus. Tears spilled out as she gazed up at him.

"This is too much, Henry. Too much."

"It isn't," came her husband's certain voice. "It is all that you deserve and more, my love. I shall devote the rest of my life to ensuring you never again receive anything less."

She did fling herself into his arms this time, and Henry caught her up in a kiss so delicious that she barely heard her son's wail as he let her know they'd been outside in the freezing winter's dawn for long enough.

Their joyful party toiled down the hill to their carriage. Another stood beside their own. Bowing, the General offered seats to their guests.

"I'm billeted at the Embassy," he explained, "but it's no trouble at all to take in any part of the city on my way."

Madame relieved Louisa of her son and stepped in at once. "I shall see you at the Hôtel Westminster, Louisa." She waved gaily as the baron helped in his lady before stepping in behind the Reverend Briscall.

Louisa allowed Henry to help her into the other carriage, still marvelling at the prettiness of Paris beneath the snow.

"I wish I had my paints," she commented.

Henry chuckled as he settled himself beside her. "Not today surely, but if you need paints, you shall have them." He placed a kiss at her temple. "You shall have everything I can give you."

Louisa leaned back and smiled at him. "I do not understand how Papa arrived here so quickly. You did not know I would agree to marry you."

Henry looked at her seriously. "I had word at the Embassy that he was en route. He left Vienna shortly after the baron and myself. The rumours regarding Bonaparte have many heads of state concerned."

"Is this why we travel to Berlin?"

Henry nodded. "Certainly, it is one reason. I know Paris is important to you—"

"*Art* is important to me. Art, my son, and you. I have no wish to be stranded in a besieged city, with an infant child and nothing but my easel and brushes to protect us. I am quite content to accompany you to Berlin. One imagines there is as much to paint there as here. Lady Rebecca will make a lovely portrait."

Henry grinned. "And I am sure von Humboldt will pay you handsomely for it. Madame has asked that you allow me to negotiate your commissions from now on."

"Madame negotiated excellently well," Louisa objected.

"A man will negotiate better," Henry pointed out. "Besides," his grin widened, "bedding your models is a habit your husband cannot encourage."

Louisa laughed. "Did you mention your modelling to Papa?"

"No chance." Henry coughed, dropping his humorous tone. "Regarding the General, I had to inform him of our betrothal. I could hardly do so without explaining the full circumstances. I want you to know, however, that I did not discuss Henri's father."

"Christmas is truly a day for miracles. I am astonished he did not object."

Henry smiled faintly. "As I wrote you, Uncle George regrets his treatment of you. He has felt this for some time. You saw his delight for yourself, I hope." He was quiet for a beat. "He's asked when I shall adopt your son."

There was another pause as Louisa studied her new husband, who seemed strangely tentative.

"What did you tell him?"

Henry looked into her eyes. "I told him that Henri's mother will decide his grandson's future and no one else." A rueful shrug accompanied this statement. "I must say, he was a little subdued after that."

"Thank you, Henry." Louisa raised her brows and took her husband's hand. "I should have liked to witness his countenance in that moment."

"I am sure it would make excellent portraiture," Henry replied. "Though he is my CO, and he did give us his blessing. There is nothing to reproach him with from this day at least." He paused. "I have requested he join us for breakfast at the Hôtel Westminster. That is if you wish to stay there with me?"

"Oh, Henry, yes. I should love nothing better."

"Excellent." His blue eyes brightened to a glow. "You ought to take Henri into the main dining room. Von Humboldt insisted they erect a fir tree, after which he had the maître d′ place paper stars and candles all over the thing. A Rhineland custom, he says. It's quite lovely, and children seem to find it fascinating. However, I doubt such an undertaking will prove popular in England or France."

"Mm, it sounds lovely." For once, she wasn't thinking of Henri. "Henry?"

"Yes, Louisa?"

"When will you wish us to—to be together as husband and wife? I mean, when shall we stay with you always?"

"Now," he growled by her ear. "Immediately."

Louisa tilted her head upward, sighing with pleasure as his mouth covered hers. Leaning back a little, she stopped his kiss so she could see his face. "Is there a reason for such haste?"

Henry pulled her scandalously close to his body until she could not mistake the feel of him. "There is, indeed." He moved his lips to her neck until wet heat bloomed between her thighs.

"Very well." She cleared her throat. "Where is *le hôtel* of yours?"

Henry teased her lips with his, stroking her thigh through her skirts. "Come here," he murmured, pulling her into his lap.

Louisa's feverish pulse returned, and she gasped as his lips tasted her mouth. Her palm moved slowly over Henry's thigh, slipping beneath his coat. He issued a soft groan as she found his heat and kept her hand there, running her fingers over him. He broke their kiss to stare at her.

"You have no idea how dangerous that is," he rasped.

"How far is it—"

"Less than ten minutes."

"Then why—"

"I'm not waiting a moment longer to make you mine," he said, peppering her face with tiny kisses.

Louisa looked into his eyes, so soft and warm and full of love. "Yes," she whispered. "I think we've both waited quite long enough."

Her Henry didn't answer—at least not with words.

Epilogue

One year later
The Christmas Salon
Berlin

Louisa walked slowly through the newest Christmas Salon with little Henri's hand clasped firmly in hers. It was slow going amid the crowds, but Henri hadn't been on his feet long, and the pace suited them.

Henry walked a little behind them, keeping an eye on Henri's tendency to fall over without warning. Stopping before the now-infamous portrait of *Madonna and Child*, Louisa gazed up at the woman she had been almost eighteen months earlier. Beside her, Henry lifted Henri into his arms as the crowds gathered to stare at the mother who showed her teeth, fed her child, and posed for the equally infamous Madame Vignée.

The newest director of Berlin's *der Weihnachtssalon* pushed through the crowds to greet them. Louisa curtsied to his bow and could not resist kissing the baron on both cheeks. Henry did his best to bow, setting Henri on his feet long enough to do the same. The baron patted the little boy's head, bowing again in return.

"It's wonderful to see you again, Wilhelm." Louisa smiled. "How is your baroness?"

Their friend's face clouded a moment. "Her lying-in was not easy, but she is recovering. I've sent her home. She is quite put out to miss the salon's opening night."

Louisa nodded. "This is understandable, but Rebecca's health is of no small moment. These crowds cannot be soothing. Your salon is well done. You must be so proud, and I understand you also have a healthy little girl?"

The baron beamed. "I thank you, Mrs Musgrave. Little Elise is quite well. You will meet her at Christmas. A playmate, perhaps, for your young man?"

"I'm sure Henri will honoured to make her acquaintance," Henry replied, scooping the boy back into his arms as the crowds pressed closer. "As soon as arrangements for the residence in Montmartre are complete, you must attend on us, as well."

"It is a shame you are no closer to the centre of Paris, is it not?" the baron lamented.

Louisa felt Henry's eyes on her. There was an excellent reason for the carriage ride between *le Louvre* and Montmartre, but it was not one she intended to discuss here. She looked at her son to hide her blush before realising the baron addressed her.

"I must thank you for the loan of your most valuable work, Madame Musgrave." The baron bowed again to Louisa, a smile playing at his lips.

Louisa hastened to correct him. "You are mistaken, Wilhelm. This is the work of Madame Vignée. Surely you are aware?"

The baron smiled. "Madame Vignée is indeed the artist. My gratitude is to the owner of the work. The major here has purchased this piece for your son. Negotiations concluded this morning." His smile broke out fully now, and Henry joined in his laughter.

"*Maman!*" shouted Henri, staring up at the framed vision of the woman he'd likely always considered his personal property.

Von Humboldt laughed again. "You are quite correct, little Henri. Allow me to show you her *Kassandra*."

The little boy looked shyly back at his mama.

"You may go with Wilhelm, Henri." Louisa nodded at him. "Mama is right here." She watched her son slip his little hand into the baron's as they moved along the aisle.

She turned to Henry. "Is this truly so, Henry? You have done this for Henri?"

"For us, dearest Louisa," Henry corrected her softly, before covering her lips with his. "*Us*, Louisa. You, me, and little Henri."

Louisa leaned back to admire the warmth in his beloved blue eyes. Her heart sang as his voice echoed the earnestness in her soul.

"I promised you a Christmas to remember," Henry reminded her. "I mean to keep that promise. Every year."

"Have you purchased any other paintings?"

"Oh yes," Henry replied with the sort of grin that hinted he'd not finished surprising her. "I am the owner of Traversant's entire catalogue, excepting the one piece gracing Wellington's walls. I shall have that too, by next Christmas. Wellington is not keen to part with it, but his lady wife would give the work away if she could. The Duchess does not like life-sized studies of divine redheads on the brink of ecstasy in her boudoir. Jealousy, you know, is an unpretty affliction."

He grinned at her. "I intend staging my own exhibition, dearest."

Louisa gasped. "You will exhibit my nudes in our home?"

Henry sank his voice in a way that never failed to ignite the insistent throb within her. "Have you not seen my new bedchamber?"

"New bedchamber?" she echoed, heat moving upward from her toes to her thighs, *and there's that throb again...*

Henry leaned toward her, touching his lips to hers once more. He tasted sweet with wine, warm with lust, and promises of more— more love, more trust, and more to come. It was a promise she trusted.

"Merry Christmas, Louisa." Her husband pressed her wrist to his lips. "I love you."

"Oh, Henry," she breathed. "Merry Christmas. I love you so much. Henri and I, we both do. Thank you for trusting me. For loving us. Thank you for *you*."

Henry laughed gently, a low, husky sound. "What else can I do, Louisa? It's *you*. It's always been you."

It was quite impossible not to kiss him after that.

HISTORICAL NOTES

The Paris Salon:

The Christmas Salon, is based on the annual Paris Salon, which is held every October, and has been in existence since 1667, in one form or another. Between 1748 and 1890, it was known as the premier art event in the Western world. Until the French Revolution, the Paris Salon was sponsored by the French nobility, under the direction of the Royal Academy of Painting and Sculpture.

In 1791, Salon sponsorship moved to that of the newly-installed government. Despite this change in support and focus, the selection of artworks remained conservative. The selection jury (established in 1748), rarely broke with the traditional themes of mythology, historical figures, and allegorical scenes. They merely pivoted their focus, swapping out imagery of the nobility for paintings of Napoleon and his fraternity posing in much the same scenarios.

Napoleon opened the Paris Salon more widely in 1804, allowing artists outside the Paris Academy (and indeed, France), to show their work. During "The Terror" that engulfed France after the revolution, part of the Louvre was damaged by riots and fire. There are references to the years without exhibits in The Christmas Salon, although the dates for this period have been fictionalised.

There is no specific art exhibition held in Paris over Christmas.

The Paris Academy:

During the French Revolution, most institutes of higher learning were suppressed as elitists, including the Paris Academy, which focused on art and sculpture. However, the Academy made a comeback in 1795 under another name. In 1803, the Emperor Napoleon reorganised these institutions to improve accessibility for those unconnected with the nobility. By April 1814 however, Bonaparte was imprisoned on Elbe, and the French royalists seemed ascendant.

After the Bourbon Restoration, the Academy was referred to as Institut Royal de France, though the name "Academy" was revived again a short while later, I chose this term as it connects more clearly with the The Paris Salon.

The Paris Academy was one of the few artistic institutions to admit female portraitists, though they only allowed four per year. Female artists were not permitted to attend life drawing classes where male nudes were present, and were expected to produce still life and landscapes, rather than figure paintings. They were also required to pay for their own classes at The Louvre, and could not compete for any of the coveted prizes at The Paris Salon.

Women were excluded from attending The Paris Academy entirely during Napoleon's reign. He had reservations regarding women's access to institutions of higher learning. Despite this, several female portraitists managed to make their mark on the art world during the English Regency era. One was Marguerite Gérard, who excelled in many painting styles for over fifty years who never married or had children.

Another notable female painter was Élisabeth Louise Vigée Le Brun, who caused a scandal in 1787 when one of her self-portraits with her daughter beside her, showed her smiling and with teeth. She was Marie Antoinette's favourite portraitist and was forced into exile during the revolution.

The Congress of Vienna:

Although Napoleon abdicated as Emperor of France in April 1814, it wasn't until July that the great nations of Europe sat down to discuss the balance of power at The Congress of Vienna. The Four Great Powers (Prussia, England, Austria, and Russia), had the most influence. As the "losing" power, France was at first not even invited. It was Talleyrand who changed this for the French, and their admittance was gained from September 1814, after much Machiavellian manoeuvring.

The Congress ushered in a century of peace for Europe (from 1814 until 1914). This was the first time such a gathering of heads of state and government had occurred in Europe, and it formed the foundation for western diplomatic discussions from that point onwards.

While there were many formal meetings held at Vienna, there were equally as many balls, dinners and entertainments. It's also worth noting that the Congress continued on in early 1815, even after the former French Emperor escaped his prison and tried again—but that's another book.

Further Reading:

British diplomacy, 1813–1815: Select Documents Dealing with the Reconstruction of Europe, G. Bell and sons Limited (1921)

Hilde Spiel: *The Congress of Vienna; An Eyewitness Account,* Chilton Book Co. Philadelphia (1968)

Thomas Crow: *Painters and Public Life in 18th Century Paris*, Yale University Press (1987)

ABOUT THE AUTHOR

Clyve Rose is an award-winning author of historical fiction in Australia and the US. She has been writing historical romance for the best part of two decades. The first piece she published was a fictional biography of an erotica writer who made a living crafting extremely explicit dating profiles for online chat sites.

Clyve lives fairly simply these days, sharing her home with a small white demon dog and a budding Amazonian warrior. She believes that love is the highest and strongest force known in the world, and that it only manifests when we are our best and truest selves. She'll continue writing about love in all its various, glorious forms, and that one day her epitaph will read *Just one more read-through*.

When she isn't writing fiction, she can be found pounding the sand at any of the beautiful beaches near her Australian home. She's addicted to short-haul ocean swims and researching quirky historical fashion trends.

CONNECT WITH CLYVE:
Website & blog: clyverose.com
Twitter: @clyverose
IG: @clyverose
FB: Clyve Rose

www.BOROUGHSPUBLISHINGGROUP.com

If you enjoyed this book, please write a review. Our authors appreciate the feedback, and it helps future readers find books they love. We welcome your comments and invite you to send them to info@boroughspublishinggroup.com. Follow us on Facebook, Twitter and Instagram, and be sure to sign up for our newsletter for surprises and new releases from your favorite authors.

Are you an aspiring writer? Check out www.boroughspublishinggroup.com/submit and see if we can help you make your dreams come true.

www.ingramcontent.com/pod-product-compliance
Lightning Source LLC
Chambersburg PA
CBHW071346170626
46811CB00003B/1009